MORAL DISORDER

BOOKS BY MARGARET ATWOOD

FICTION

The Edible Woman

Surfacing

Lady Oracle

Dancing Girls

Life Before Man

Bodily Harm

Murder in the Dark

Bluebeard's Egg

The Handmaid's Tale

Cat's Eye

Wilderness Tips

Good Bones

The Robber Bride

Alias Grace

The Blind Assassin

Good Bones and Simple Murders

Oryx and Crake

The Penelopiad

The Tent

Moral Disorder

FOR CHILDREN

Up in the Tree

Anna's Pet (with Joyce Barkhouse)

For the Birds

Princess Prunella and the Purple Peanut

Rude Ramsay and the Roaring Radishes

Bashful Bob and Doleful Dorinda

MORAL DISORDER

stories

Margaret Atwood

Nan A. Talese
DOUBLEDAY
New York London Toronto Sydney Auckland

PUBLISHED BY NAN A. TALESE
AN IMPRINT OF DOUBLEDAY

Published in the United States by Nan A. Talese, an imprint of The Doubleday
Broadway Publishing Group, a division of Random House, Inc., New York.

DOUBLEDAY is a registered trademark of Random House, Inc.

BOOK DESIGN BY AMANDA DEWEY

ISBN-13: 978-0-7394-8149-3

PRINTED IN THE UNITED STATES OF AMERICA

For my family

Contents

The Bad News

It's morning. For now, night is over. It's time for the bad news. I think of the bad news as a huge bird, with the wings of a crow and the face of my Grade Four schoolteacher, sparse bun, rancid teeth, wrinkly frown, pursed mouth and all, sailing around the world under cover of darkness, pleased to be the bearer of ill tidings, carrying a basket of rotten eggs, and knowing – as the sun comes up – exactly where to drop them. On me, for one.

At our place, the bad news arrives in the form of the bad-news paper. Tig carries it up the stairs. Tig's real name is Gilbert. It's impossible to explain nicknames to speakers of foreign languages, not that I have to do this much.

"They just killed the leader of the interim governing council," Tig announces. It's not that he's impervious to bad news: on the contrary. He's angular, he has less body fat than I do and therefore less capacity to absorb, to cushion, to turn the calories of bad news — and it does have calories, it raises your blood pressure — into the substance of his own body. I can do that, he can't. He wants to pass the bad news on as soon as possible — get it off his hands, like a hot potato. Bad news burns him.

I'm still in bed. I'm not really awake. I was doing a little wallowing. I was enjoying this morning until now. "Not before breakfast," I say. I do not add, "You know I can't handle it this early in the day." I've added that before; it's had only an intermittent effect. After this long together, both of our heads are filled with such minor admonitions, helpful hints about the other person — likes and dislikes, preferences and taboos. Don't come up behind me like that when I'm reading. Don't use my kitchen knives. Don't just strew things. Each believes the other should respect this frequently reiterated set of how-to instructions, but they cancel each other out: if Tig must respect my need to wallow mindlessly, free of bad news, before the first cup of coffee, shouldn't I respect his need to spew out catastrophe so he himself will be rid of it?

"Oh. Sorry," he says. He shoots me a reproachful look. Why must I disappoint him like this? Don't I know that if he can't tell the bad news, to me, right now, some bilious green bad-news gland or bladder inside him will burst and he'll get peritonitis of the soul? Then I'll be sorry.

He's right, I would be sorry. I'd have no one left whose mind I can read.

"I'm getting up now," I say, hoping I sound comforting. "I'll be right down."

"Now" and "right down" don't have the same meaning they used to have. Everything takes longer than it did back then. But I can still

THE BAD NEWS

get through the routine, out of the nightdress, into the day dress, the doing-up of the shoes, the lubrication of the face, the selection of the vitamin pills. The leader, I think. The interim governing council. Killed by *them*. A year from now I won't remember which leader, which interim governing council, which them. But such items multiply. Everything is interim, no one can govern any more, and there are lots of them, of thems. They always want to kill the leaders. With the best of intentions, or so they claim. The leaders have the best of intentions as well. The leaders stand in the spotlight, the killers aim from the dark; it's easy to score.

As for the other leaders, the leaders of the leading countries, as they're called, those aren't really leading any more, they're flailing around; you can see it in their eyes, white-rimmed like the eyes of panic-stricken cattle. You can't lead if no one will follow. People throw up their hands, then sit on them. They just want to get on with their lives. The leaders keep saying, "We need strong leader-ship," then they sneak off to peek at their poll ratings. It's the bad news, there's too much of it: they can't take it.

But there's been bad news before, and we got through it. That's what people say, about things that happened before they were born, or while they were still thumb-sucking. I love this formulation: *We got through it*. It means dick shit when it's about any event you per-sonally weren't there for, as if you'd joined some *We* club, pinned on some tacky plastic *We* badge, to qualify. Still, *We got through it* — that's bracing. It conjures up a march or a procession, horses pranc-ing, costumes tattered and muddied because of the siege or battle or enemy occupation or butchering of dragons or forty-year trek through the wilderness. There'd be a bearded leader hoisting his standard and pointing forward. The leader would have got the bad news early. He'd got it, he'd understood it, he'd known what to do.

Attack from the flank! Go for the throat! Get the hell out of Egypt! That sort of thing.

"Where are you?" Tig calls up the stairs. "Coffee's ready."

"I'm here," I call back down. We use this a lot, this walkie-talkie of air. Communication hasn't failed us, not yet. *Not yet* is aspirated, like the *h* in *honour*. It's the silent *not yet*. We don't say it out loud.

These are the tenses that define us now: past tense, *back then*; future tense, *not yet*. We live in the small window between them, the space we've only recently come to think of as *still*, and really it's no smaller than anyone else's window. True, there are little things going wrong with us – a knee here, an eye there – but so far just little things. We can still enjoy ourselves, as long as we focus on doing one item at a time. I can remember when I used to tease our daughter, back then, when she was an adolescent. I'd do it by pretending to be old. I'd bump into walls, drop cutlery, fake memory loss. Then we'd both laugh. It's no longer such a joke.

Our now-dead cat, Drumlin, developed cat senility when she was seventeen. Drumlin – why did we call her that? The other cat, the one that died first, was Moraine. Once we thought it was amusing to name our cats after glacial-dump geological features, though the point of it escapes me now. Tig said that Drumlin ought to have been named Landfill Site, but he was the one whose job it was to empty her litter box.

It's not likely we will have another cat. I used to think – I thought this quite calmly – that after Tig was gone (for men die first, don't they?) I might get a cat again, for company. I no longer consider this an option. I'll surely be half-blind by then, and a cat might run between my legs, and I'd trip over it and break my neck.

Poor Drumlin used to prowl the house at night, yowling in an unearthly fashion. Nothing gave her solace: she was looking for

THE BAD NEWS

something she'd lost, though she didn't know what it was. (Her mind, in point of fact, if cats can be said to have minds.) In the mornings we'd find small bites taken out of tomatoes, of pears: she'd forgotten she was a carnivore, she'd forgotten what it was she was supposed to eat. This has become my picture of my future self: wandering the house in the darkness, in my white nightdress, howling for what I can't quite remember I've lost. It's unbearable. I wake up in the night and reach out to make sure Tig is still there, still breathing. So far, so good.

The kitchen, when I get to it, smells like toast and coffee: not surprising, because that's what Tig has been making. The smell wraps around me like a blanket, stays there while I eat the actual toast and drink the actual coffee. There, on the table, is the bad news.

"The refrigerator's been making a noise," I say. We don't pay enough attention to our appliances. Neither of us do. Stuck on to the refrigerator is a photo of our daughter, taken several years ago; it beams down on us like the light from a receding star. She's busy with her own life, elsewhere.

"Look at the paper," says Tig.

There are pictures. Is bad news worse with pictures? I think so. Pictures make you look, whether you want to or not. There's the burnt-out car, one of a series by now, with its skeletal frame of twisted metal. A charred shadow crouches inside. In pictures like these there are always empty shoes. It's the shoes that get to me. Sad, that innocent daily task – putting your shoes on your feet, in the firm belief that you'll be going somewhere.

We don't like bad news, but we need it. We need to know about it in case it's coming our way. Herd of deer in the meadow, heads down grazing peacefully. Then *woof woof* – wild dogs in the woods. Heads up, ears forward. Prepare to flee! Or the muskox defence:

wolves approaching is the news. Quick – into a circle! Females and young to the centre! Snort and paw the ground! Prepare to horn the enemy!

"They won't stop," says Tig.

"It's a mess," I say. "I wonder where the security was?" When God was handing out the brains, they used to say back then, some folks we could name were last in line.

"If someone really wants to kill you, they'll kill you," Tig says. He's a fatalist that way. I disagree, and we spend a pleasant quarter of an hour calling up our dead witnesses. He submits Archduke Ferdinand and John Kennedy; I offer Queen Victoria (eight failed attempts) and Joseph Stalin, who managed to avoid assassination by doing it wholesale himself. Once, this might have been an argument. Now it's a pastime, like gin rummy.

"We're lucky," says Tig. I know what he means. He means the two of us, sitting here in the kitchen, still. Neither of us gone. Not yet.

"Yes, we are," I say. "Watch the toast – it's burning."

There. We've dealt with the bad news, we've faced it head on, and we're all right. We have no wounds, no blood pours out of us, we aren't scorched. We have all of our shoes. The sun is shining, the birds are singing, there's no reason not to feel pretty good. The bad news comes from so far away, most of the time – the explosions, the oil spills, the genocides, the famines, all of that. There will be other news, later. There always is. We'll worry about it when it comes.

Some years ago – when? – Tig and I were in the south of France, at a place called Glanum. We were on a vacation of sorts. What we really wanted to see was the asylum where Van Gogh painted the irises, and we did see that. Glanum was a side trip. I haven't thought about it in years, but I find myself there now, back then, in Glanum, before it was destroyed in the third century, before it was only a few ruins you pay to get into.

There are spacious villas in Glanum; there are public baths, amphitheatres, temples, the kinds of buildings the Romans put up wherever they went so they could feel civilized and at home. Glanum is very pleasant; a lot of upper-level army men retire here. It's quite multicultural, quite diverse: we're fond of novelty, of the exotic, though not so much as they are in Rome. We're a bit provincial here. Still, we have gods from everywhere, in addition to the official gods, of course. For instance, we have a little temple to Cybele, decorated with two ears in token of the body part you might wish to cut off in her honour. The men make jokes about that: you're lucky to get away with just the ears, they say. Better an earless man than no man at all.

There are older Greek houses mixed in with the Roman ones, and a few Greek ways linger still. Celts come to town; some of them wear tunics and cloaks like ours, and speak decent Latin. Our relations with them are friendly enough, now that they've renounced their headhunting ways. Tig has to do a certain amount of entertaining, and I once invited a leading Celt to dinner. It was a social risk, though a minor one: our guest behaved normally enough, and got just as drunk as manners required. His hair was odd — reddish and curly — and he was wearing his ceremonial bronze torque, but he was no more ferocious than some other men I might name, though he did have an eerie politeness.

I'm having my breakfast, in the morning room with the mural of Pomona and the Zephyrs. The painter was not first-rate — Pomona is slightly walleyed and her breasts are enormous, but you can't always get first-rate here. What would I be eating? Bread, honey, dried figs. Fresh fruit isn't in season yet. No coffee, worse luck; I don't think it's been invented yet. I'm having some fermented mare's milk, as an aid to digestion. A faithful slave has brought the breakfast in on a silver tray. They're good at slavery on this estate, they do it well: they're silent, discreet, efficient. They don't want to be sold, naturally: being a house-slave is better than working in the quarry.

Tig comes in with a scroll. Tig is short for Tigris, a nickname bestowed on him by his erstwhile troops. Only a few intimates call him Tig. He's frowning.

"Bad news?" I ask.

"The barbarians are invading," he says. "They've crossed the Rhine."

"Not before breakfast," I say. He knows I can't discuss weighty matters right after getting up. But I've been too abrupt: I see his stricken look, and I relent. "They're always crossing the Rhine. You'd think they'd get tired of it. Our legions will defeat them. They always have before."

"I don't know," says Tig. "We shouldn't have let so many barbarians into the army. You can't depend on them." He spent a long time in the army himself, so his worry means something. On the other hand, it's his general view that Rome is going to hell in a handcart, and I've noticed that most retired men feel like that: the world simply cannot function minus their services. It's not that they feel useless; they feel unused.

"Please, sit down," I say. "I'll order you a nice piece of bread and honey, with figs." Tig sits down. I don't proffer the mare's milk, though it would do him good. He knows I know he doesn't like it. He hates being nagged about his health, which has been giving him some problems lately. Oh, make things stay the way they are, I pray to him silently.

THE BAD NEWS

"Did you hear?" I say. "They found a freshly cut-off head, hung up beside the old Celtic votive well." Some escaped quarry worker who ran off into the woods, which they've been warned against, heaven knows. "Do you think they're reverting to paganism? The Celts?"

"They hate us, really," says Tig. "That memorial arch doesn't help. It's hardly tactful – Celts being defeated, Roman feet on their heads. Haven't you caught them staring at our necks? They'd love to stick the knife in. But they're soft now, they're used to luxuries. Not like the northern barbarians. The Celts know that if we go under, they'll go under too."

He takes only one bite of the lovely bread. Then he stands up, paces around. He looks flushed. "I'm going to the baths," he says. "For the news."

Gossip and rumour, I think. Portents, forebodings; birds in flight, sheep's entrails. You never know if the news is true until it pounces. Until it's right on top of you. Until you reach out in the night and there's no more breathing. Until you're howling in darkness, wandering the empty rooms, in your white dress.

"We'll get through it," I say. Tig says nothing.

It's such a beautiful day. The air smells of thyme, the fruit trees are in flower. But this means nothing to the barbarians; in fact, they prefer to invade on beautiful days. It provides more visibility for their lootings and massacres. These are the same barbarians who – I've heard – fill wicker cages with victims and set them on fire as a sacrifice to their gods. Still, they're very far away. Even if they manage to cross the Rhine, even if they aren't slain in thousands, even if the river fails to run red with their blood, they won't get here for a long time. Not in our lifetime, perhaps. Glanum is in no danger, not yet.

The Art of Cooking
and Serving

The summer I was eleven I spent a lot of time knitting. I knitted doggedly, silently, crouched over the balls of wool and the steel needles and the lengthening swath of knitwear in a posture that was far from easy. I'd learned to knit too early in life to have mastered the trick of twisting the strand around my index finger – the finger had been too short – so I had to jab the right-hand needle in, hold it there with two left-hand fingers, then lift the entire right hand to loop the wool around the tip of the needle. I'd seen women who were able to knit and talk at the same time, barely glancing down, but I couldn't do it that way. My style of knitting required total concentration and caused my arms to ache, and irritated me a lot.

What I was knitting was a layette. A layette was a set of baby garments you were supposed to dress the newborn baby in so it would be warm when it was brought home from the hospital. At the very least you needed to have two thumbless mittens, two stubby booties, a pair of leggings, a jacket, and a bonnet, to which you could add a knitted blanket if you had the patience, as well as a thing called a soaker. The soaker looked like a pair of shorts with pumpkin-shaped legs, like the ones in pictures of Sir Francis Drake. Cloth diapers and rubber baby pants were prone to leaks: that's what the soaker was for. But I was not going to knit the soaker. I hadn't yet got around to visualizing the fountains, the streams, the rivers of pee a baby was likely to produce.

The blanket was tempting – there was one with rabbits on it that I longed to create – but I knew I had to draw the line somewhere because I didn't have all the time in the world. If I dawdled, the baby might arrive before I was ready for it and be forced to wear some sort of mismatched outfit put together out of hand-me-downs. I'd started on the leggings and the mittens, as being fairly simple – mostly alternate rows of knit and purl, with some ribbing thrown in. That way I could work up to the jacket, which was more complicated. I was saving the bonnet to the last: it was going to be my *chef-d'oeuvre*. It was to be ornamented with satin ribbons to tie under the baby's chin – the possibilities of strangulation through ties like this had not yet been considered – and with huge ribbon rosettes that would stick out on either side of the baby's face like small cabbages. Babies dressed in layettes, I knew from the pictures in the Beehive pattern book, were supposed to resemble confectionary – clean and sweet, delicious little cakelike bundles decorated with pastel icing.

The colour I'd chosen was white. It was the orthodox colour, though a few of the Beehive patterns were shown in an elfin pale green or a practical yellow. But white was best: after it was known whether the baby was a boy or a girl I could add the ribbons, blue or pink. I had a vision of how the entire set would look when finished – pristine, gleaming, admirable, a tribute to my own goodwill and kindness. I hadn't yet realized it might also be a substitute for them.

I was knitting this layette because my mother was expecting. I avoided the word *pregnant*, as did others: *pregnant* was a blunt, bulgy, pendulous word, it weighed you down to think about it, whereas *expecting* suggested a dog with its ears pricked, listening briskly and with happy anticipation to an approaching footstep. My mother was old for such a thing: I'd gathered this by eavesdropping while she talked with her friends in the city, and from the worried wrinkles on the foreheads of the friends, and from their compressed lips and tiny shakes of the head, and from their *Oh dear* tone, and from my mother saying she would just have to make the best of it. I gathered that something might be wrong with the baby because of my mother's age; but wrong how, exactly? I listened as much as I could, but I couldn't make it out, and there was no one I could ask. Would it have no hands, would it have a little pinhead, would it be a moron? *Moron* was a term of abuse, at school. I wasn't sure what it meant, but there were children you weren't supposed to stare at on the street, because it wasn't their fault, they had just been born that way.

I'd been told about the expectant state of my mother in May, by my father. It had made me very anxious, partly because I'd also been told that until my new baby brother or sister had arrived safely my mother would be in a dangerous condition. Something terrible might happen to her – something that might make her very ill – and it was all the more likely to happen if I myself did not pay proper attention. My father did not say what this thing was, but his gravity and terseness meant that it was a serious business.

My mother – said my father – was not supposed to sweep the floor, or carry anything heavy such as pails of water, or bend down much, or lift bulky objects. We would all have to pitch in, said my father, and do extra tasks. It would be my brother's job to mow the lawn, from now until June, when we would go up north. (Up north there was no lawn. In any case my brother wouldn't be there: he was heading off to a camp for boys, to do things with axes in the woods.) As for me, I would just have to be generally helpful. More helpful than usual, my father added in a manner that was meant to be encouraging. He himself would be helpful too, of course. But he couldn't be there all the time. He had some work to do, when we would be at what other people called *the cottage* but we called *the island*. (Cottages had iceboxes and gas generators and water-skiing, all of which we lacked.) It was necessary for him to be away, which was unfortunate, he continued. But he would not be gone for very long, and he was sure I would be up to it.

I myself was not so sure. He always thought I knew more than I knew, and that I was bigger than I was, and older, and hardier. What he mistook for calmness and competence was actually fright: that was why I stared at him in silence, nodding my head. The danger that loomed was so vague, and therefore so large – how could I even prepare for it? At the back of my mind, my feat of knitting was a sort of charm, like the fairy-tale suits of nettles mute princesses were supposed to make for their swan-shaped brothers, to turn them back into human beings. If I could only complete the full set of baby garments, the baby that was supposed to fit inside them would be conjured into the world, and thus out of my mother. Once outside, where I could see it – once it had a face – it could be dealt with. As it was, the thing was a menace.

Thus I knitted on, with single-minded concentration. I finished the mittens before we went up north; they were more or less flawless, except for the odd botched stitch. After I got to the island, I polished off the leggings – the leg that was shorter could be stretched, I felt. Without pause I started on the jacket, which was to have several bands of seed stitch on it – a challenge, but one I was determined to overcome.

Meanwhile my mother was being no use at all. At the beginning of my knitting marathon she'd undertaken to do the booties. She did know how to knit, she'd knitted in the past: the pattern book I was using had once been hers. She could turn heels, a skill I hadn't quite mastered. But despite her superior ability, she was slacking off: all she'd done so far was half a bootie. Her knitting lay neglected while she rested in a deck chair, her feet up on a log, reading historical romances with horseback riding and poisoning and swordplay in them – I knew, I'd read them myself – or else just dozing, her head lying slackly on a pillow, her face pale and moist, her hair damp and lank, her stomach sticking out in a way that made me feel dizzy, as I did when someone else had cut their finger. She'd taken to wearing an old smock she'd put away in a trunk, long ago; I remembered using it for dressing up at Halloween once, when I was being a fat lady with a purse. It made her look poor.

It was scary to watch her sleeping in the middle of the day. It was unlike her. Normally she was a person who went for swift, purposeful walks, or skated around rinks in winter at an impressive speed, or swam with a lot of kicking, or rattled up the dishes – she called it rattling them up. She always knew what to do in an emergency, she was methodical and cheerful, she took command. Now it was if she had abdicated.

THE ART OF COOKING AND SERVING

When I wasn't knitting, I swept the floor diligently. I pumped out pails and pails of water with the hand pump and lugged them up the hill one at a time, spilling water down my bare legs; I did the washing in the zinc washtub, scrubbing the clothes with Sunlight soap on the washboard, carting them down to the lake to rinse them out, hauling them up the hill again to hang them on the line. I weeded the garden, I carried in the wood, all against the background of my mother's alarming passivity.

Once a day she went for a swim, although she didn't swim energetically, not the way she used to, she just floated around; and I would go in too, whether I wanted to or not: I had to prevent her from drowning. I had a fear of her sinking down suddenly, down through the cold brownish water, with her hair fanning out like seaweed and her eyes gazing solemnly up at me. In that case I would have to dive down and get my arm around her neck and tow her to shore, but how could I do that? She was so big. But nothing like that had happened yet, and she liked going into the water; it seemed to wake her up. With only her head sticking out, she looked more like herself. At such times she would even smile, and I would have the illusion that everything was once again the way it was supposed to be.

But then she would emerge, dripping – there were varicose veins on the backs of her legs, I couldn't avoid seeing them, although they embarrassed me – and make her way with painful slowness up to our cabin, and put together our lunch. The lunch would be sardines, or peanut butter on crackers, or cheese if we had any, and tomatoes from the garden, and carrots I'd dug out and washed. She didn't appear much interested in eating this lunch, but she chewed away at it anyway. She would make an effort at conversation – how was my knitting coming along? – but I didn't know what to say to her. I couldn't understand why she'd chosen to do what she'd done – why she'd turned herself into this listless, bloated version of herself, thus changing the future – my future – into something shadow-filled and uncertain. I thought she'd done it on purpose. It didn't occur to me that she might have been ambushed.

It was mid-August: hot and oppressive. The cicadas sang in the trees, the dry pine needles crackled underfoot. The lake was ominously still, the way it was when thunder was gathering. My mother was dozing. I sat on the dock, slapping at the stable flies and worrying. I felt like crying, but I could not allow myself to do that. I was completely alone. What would I do if the dangerous thing – whatever it was – began to happen? I thought I knew what it might be: the baby would start to come out, too soon. And then what? I couldn't exactly stuff it back in.

We were on an island, there were no other people in sight, there was no telephone, it was seven miles by boat to the nearest village. I would have to start the outboard motor on our clunky old boat – I knew how to do this, though pulling the cord hard enough was almost beyond my strength – and go all the way to the village, which could take an hour. From there I could telephone for help. But what if the motor wouldn't start? That had been known to happen. Or what if it broke down on the way? There was a tool kit, but I'd learned only the most elementary operations. I could fix a shear pin, I could check a gas line; if those things didn't work I would have to row, or wave and yell at passing fishermen, if any.

Or I could use the canoe – put a stone in the stern to weight it down, paddle from the bow end, as I'd been taught. But that method would be useless in a wind, even a light wind: I wasn't strong enough to hold a course, I would be blown sideways.

THE ART OF COOKING AND SERVING

I thought of a plan of last resort. I would take the canoe over to one of the small offshore islands – I could get that far, no matter what. Then I would set fire to the island. The smoke would be seen by a fire ranger, who would send a float plane, and I would stand on the dock in full view and jump up and down and wave a white pillowcase. This could not fail. The risk was that I would set the mainland on fire as well, by accident. Then I would end up in jail as an arsonist. But I would just have to do it anyway. It was either that, or my mother would . . . Would what?

Here my mind cut out, and I ran up the hill and walked softly past my sleeping mother and into the cabin, and got out the jar full of raisins, and made my way to the large poplar tree where I always went when I'd come to the edge of an unthinkable thought. I propped myself against the tree, crammed a handful of raisins into my mouth, and plunged into my favourite book.

This book was a cookbook. It was called *The Art of Cooking and Serving*, and I'd recently thrown over all novels and even *The Guide to Woodland Mushrooms* and devoted myself to it entirely. It was by a woman called Sarah Field Splint, a name I trusted. *Sarah* was old-fashioned and dependable, *Field* was pastoral and flowery, and *Splint* – well, there could be no nonsense and weeping and hysteria and doubts about the right course of action with a woman called Splint by your side. This book dated from the olden days, ten years before I was born; it had been put out by the Crisco company, a manufacturer of vegetable shortening, at the beginning of the Depression, when butter had become expensive – said my mother – so all the recipes in it had Crisco in them. We always had lots of Crisco on the island, because butter went bad in the heat. Crisco on the other hand was virtually indestructible. In the long ago, before she'd started expecting, my mother had used it to make pies, and her writing could be found here and there among the recipes: *Good!!* she'd written. Or, *Use half white, half brown.*

It wasn't the recipes that held me in thrall, however. It was the two chapters at the front of the book. The first was called "The Servantless House," the second "The House with a Servant." Both of them were windows into another world, and I peered through them eagerly. I knew they were windows, not doors: I couldn't get in. But what entrancing lives were being lived in there!

Sarah Field Splint had strict ideas on the proper conduct of life. She had rules, she imposed order. Hot foods must be served *hot*, cold foods *cold*. "It just *has* to be done, however it is accomplished," she said. That was the kind of advice I needed to hear. She was firm on the subject of clean linen and shining silver. "Better never to use anything but doilies, and keep *them* immaculately fresh, than to cover the table for even one meal with a cloth having a single spot on it," she ordered. We had oilcloth on our table, and stainless steel. As for doilies, they were something beyond my experience, but I thought it would be elegant to have some.

Despite her insistence on the basics, Sarah Field Splint had other, more flexible values. Mealtimes must be enjoyed; they must have charm. Every table must have a centrepiece: a few flowers, an arrangement of fruits. Failing that, "some tiny ferns combined with a bit of partridge vine or other coloured woodsy thing in a low bowl or delicate wicker basket" would do the trick.

How I longed for a breakfast tray with a couple of daffodils in a bud vase, as pictured, or a tea table at which to entertain "a few choice friends" – who would these friends be? – or, best of all, breakfast served on a side porch, with a lovely view of "the winding river and the white church spire sailing out of the trees on the opposite bank." *Sailing* – I liked that. It sounded so peaceful.

All of these things were available to the house with no servant. Then came the servant chapter. Here too Mrs. Splint was fastidious, and solidly informative. (You could tell she was *Mrs.* Splint; she was married, though without sloppy consequences, unlike my mother.) "One can transform an untidy, inexperienced girl into a well-groomed, professional servant if one is patient and kind and fair," she told me. *Transform* was the word I seized on. Did I want to transform, or to be transformed? Was I to be the kind homemaker, or the formerly untidy maid? I hardly knew.

There were two photographs of the maid, one in daytime dress, with white shoes and stockings and a white muslin apron — what was muslin? — and the other in an afternoon tea and dinner outfit, with black stockings and organdy collar and cuffs. Her expression in both pictures was the same: a gentle little half-smile, a straight-ahead, frank, but reserved gaze, as if she was waiting for instructions. There were faint dark circles under her eyes. I couldn't tell whether she looked amiable, or put-upon, or merely stupefied. She'd be the one to get blamed if there was a spot on the tablecloth or a piece of silver less than gleaming. All the same, I envied her. She was already transformed, and had no more decisions to make.

I finished the raisins, closed the book, wiped my sticky hands on my shorts. Now it was time for more knitting. Sometimes I forgot to wash my hands and got brown raisin stains on the white wool, but that could be corrected later. Ivory Soap was what Mrs. Splint always used; it was good to know such a thing. First I went down to the garden and broke off some pea vine and a handful of red flowers from the scarlet runner beans, for the centrepiece it was now my duty to arrange. The charm of my centrepiece would not however cancel out the shabbiness of our paper napkins: my mother insisted they be used at least twice, to avoid waste, and she wrote our initials on them in pencil. I could imagine what Mrs. Splint would think of this grubby practice.

How long did all of this go on? It seemed forever, but perhaps it was only a week or two. In due course my father returned; a few maple leaves turned orange, and then a few more; the loons gathered together, calling at night before their fall migration. Soon enough we went back to the city, and I could go to school again in the normal way.

I'd finished the layette, all except the one bootie that was the responsibility of my mother — would the baby have the foot of a swan? — and I wrapped it in white tissue paper and put it in a drawer. It was a bit lopsided and not entirely clean — the raisin smears lingered — but you couldn't tell that when it was folded.

My baby sister was born in October, a couple of weeks before I turned twelve. She had all the right fingers and toes. I threaded the pink ribbon into the eyelets in the layette and sewed together the rosettes for the bonnet, and the baby came home from the hospital in the proper manner and style. My mother's friends came over to visit, and admired my handiwork, or so it appeared. "You did all this?" they said. "Almost all," I said modestly. I didn't mention my mother's failure to complete her own minor task.

My mother said she'd hardly had to lift a finger, I'd gone at the knitting just like a beaver. "What a good little worker," said the friends; but I got the impression they thought it was funny.

The baby was cute, though in no time flat she outgrew my layette. But she didn't sleep. As soon as you put her down she'd be wide awake and wailing: the clouds of anxiety that had surrounded her before she was born seemed to have entered into her, and she would wake up six or seven or eight or nine times a night, crying plaintively. This didn't go away in a few months, as Dr. Spock's *Baby and Child Care* said it would. If anything, it got worse.

From having been too fat, my mother now became too thin. She was gaunt from lack of sleep, her hair dull, her eyes bruised-looking, her shoulders hunched over. I did my homework lying on my back with my feet up on the baby's crib, jiggling it and jiggling it so my mother could get some rest. Or I would come home from school and change the baby and bundle her up and take her out in her pram, or I would pace back and forth, pressing her warm, fragrant, wriggling flannelette body against my shoulder with one hand while holding a book up with the other, or I would take her into my room and rock her in my arms and sing to her. Singing was particularly effective. *Oh my darling Nellie Gray, they have taken you away, and I'll never see my darling any more*, I would sing. Or else the "Coventry Carol" from junior choir:

> *Herod the King, in his raging,*
> *Charged he hath this day,*
> *His men of might, in his own sight,*
> *All children young, to slay.*

The tune was mournful, but it put her right to sleep.

When I wasn't doing those things, I had to clean the bathroom or do the dishes.

My sister turned one, I became thirteen; now I was in high school. She turned two, I became fourteen. My girlfriends at school – some of them were fifteen already – were loitering on the way home, talking to boys. Some of them went to the movies, where they picked up boys from other schools; others did the same at skating rinks. They exchanged views on which boys were real dolls and which were pills, they went to drive-ins on double dates with their new steadies and ate popcorn and rolled around in the back seats of cars, they tried on strapless dresses, they attended dances where, drowning in swoony music and the blue light of darkened gymnasiums, they shuffled around mashed up against their partners, they necked on the couch in their rec rooms with the TV on.

I listened to the descriptions of all this at lunch hour, but I couldn't join in. I avoided the boys who approached me: somehow I had to turn away, I had to go home and look after the baby, who was still not sleeping. My mother dragged around the house as if she was ill, or starving. She'd been to the doctor about the baby's sleeplessness, but he'd been no help. All he said was, "You've got one of *those*."

From being worried, I now became surly. I escaped from the dinner table every night as soon as I could, I shut myself in my room and answered questions from my parents with grudging mono-syllables. When I wasn't doing homework or chores or baby-tending I would lie on my bed with my head hanging over the edge, holding up a mirror to see what I looked like upside down.

One evening I was standing behind my mother. I must have been waiting for her to get out of the bathroom so I could try out something or other on myself, a different shampoo most likely. She was bending over the laundry hamper, hauling out the dirty clothes. The baby started to cry. "Could you go and put her to sleep?" she said, as she had done so often. Ordinary, I would trudge off, soothe, sing, rock.

"Why should I?" I said. "She's not *my* baby. I didn't have her. You did." I'd never said anything this rude to her. Even as the words were coming out of my mouth I knew I'd gone too far, though all I'd done was spoken the truth, or part of it.

My mother stood up and whirled around, all in one movement, and slapped me hard across the face. She'd never done that before, or anything remotely like it. I didn't say anything. She didn't say anything. We were both shocked by ourselves, and also by each other.

I ought to have felt hurt, and I did. But I also felt set free, as if released from an enchantment. I was no longer compelled to do service. On the outside, I would still be helpful — I wouldn't be able to change that about myself. But another, more secret life spread out before me, unrolling like dark fabric. I too would soon go to the drive-in theatres, I too would eat popcorn. Already in spirit I was off and running — to the movies, to the skating rinks, to the swooning blue-lit dances, and to all sorts of other seductive and tawdry and frightening pleasures I could not yet begin to imagine.

The Headless Horseman

For Halloween that year – the year my sister was two – I dressed up as the Headless Horseman. Before, I'd only ever been ghosts and fat ladies, both of which were easy: all you needed was a sheet and a lot of talcum powder, or a dress and a hat and some padding. But this year would be the last one I'd ever be able to disguise myself, or so I believed. I was getting too old for it – I was almost finished with being thirteen – and so I felt the urge to make a special effort.

Halloween was my best holiday. Why did I like it so much? Perhaps because I could take time off from being myself, or from the impersonation of myself I was finding it increasingly expedient, but also increasingly burdensome, to perform in public.

I got the Headless Horseman idea from a story we'd read in school. In the story, the Headless Horseman was a grisly legend and also a joke, and that was the effect I was aiming for. I thought every-one would be familiar with this figure: if I'd studied a thing in school I assumed it was general knowledge. I hadn't yet discovered that I lived in a sort of transparent balloon, drifting over the world without making much contact with it, and that the people I knew appeared to me at a different angle from the one at which they appeared to them-selves; and that the reverse was also true. I was smaller to others, up there in my balloon, than I was to myself. I was also blurrier.

I had an image of how the Headless Horseman was supposed to look. He was said to ride around at night with nothing on top of his shoulders but a neck, his head held in one arm, the eyes fixing the horrified viewer in a ghastly glare. I made the head out of papier mâché, using strips of newspaper soaked in a flour-and-water paste I cooked myself, as per the instructions in *The Rainy Day Book of Hobbies*. Earlier in my life – long ago, at least two years ago – I'd had a wistful desire to make all the things suggested in this book: animals twisted out of pipe cleaners, balsa-wood boats that would whiz around when you dropped cooking oil into a hole in the middle, and a tractor thing put together out of an empty thread spool, two matchsticks, and a rubber band; but somehow I could never find the right materials in our house. Cooking up paste glue was simple, however: all you needed was flour and water. Then you simmered and stirred until the paste was translucent. The lumps didn't matter, you could squeeze them out later. The glue got quite hard when it was dry, and I realized the next morning that I should have filled the pot with water after using it. My mother always said, "A good cook does her own dishes." But then, I reflected, glue was not real cooking.

The head came out too square. I squashed it at the top to make it more like a head, then left it down by the furnace to dry. The drying took longer than I'd planned, and during the process the nose shrank and the head began to smell funny. I could see that I should have spent more time on the chin, but it was too late to add on to it. When the head was dry enough, at least on the outside, I painted it what I hoped was a flesh colour – a wishy-washy bathrobe pink – and then I painted two very white eyeballs with black pupils. The eyes came out a little crossed, but it couldn't be helped: I didn't want to make the eyeballs grey by fooling around with the black pupils on the damp white paint. I added dark circles under the eyes, and black eyebrows, and black enamel hair that appeared to have been slicked down with brilliantine. I painted a red mouth, with a trickle of shiny enamel blood coming down from one corner. I'd taken care to put a neck stub on the bottom of the head, and I painted this red – for where the head had been severed – with a white circle in the middle of the bottom part, for the neck bone.

The body of the Horseman took some thought. I made a cape out of a piece of black fabric left over from a now-obsolete puppet stage of mine, gathering it at the neck end – designed to sit on top of my head – and sewing buttons down the front, and cutting two inconspicuous holes at eye level so I'd be able to see out. I borrowed my mother's jodhpurs and riding boots, left over from before she was married – she hadn't ridden a horse since her wedding day, she was in the habit of saying, proudly or regretfully. Probably it was both. But I didn't pay much attention to my mother's tone of voice, then: I had to tune it out in order to charge full speed ahead with what I myself was doing.

The riding boots were too big, but I made up for that with hockey socks. I safety-pinned the jodhpurs around the waist to keep them from falling down. I got hold of some black winter gloves, and improvised a horse whip out of a stick and a piece of leather I'd scrounged from the box of archery materials. Archery had once been popular with my father, and then with my brother; but my father had given it up, and the box had been abandoned in the trunk room in the cellar, now that my brother had to study so much.

I tried on the entire outfit in front of my mirror, with the head held in the crook of my arm. I could scarcely see myself through the eyeholes, but the dark shape looming in the glass, with two sinister eyeballs staring out balefully from somewhere near the elbow, looked pretty good to me.

On the night itself I groped my way out the door and joined my best friend of the moment, whose name was Annie. Annie had done herself up as Raggedy Ann, complete with a wig of red wool braids. We'd taken flashlights, but Annie had to hold my arm to guide me through the darker patches of the night, which were numerous in the badly lit suburb we were traversing. I should have made the eyeholes bigger.

We went from door to door, shouting, "Shell out! Shell out!" and collecting popcorn balls and candy apples and licorice twists, and the Halloween toffees wrapped in orange and black waxed paper with designs of pumpkins and bats on them of which I was especially fond. I loved the sensation of prowling abroad in the darkness – of being unseen, unknown, potentially terrifying, though all the time retaining, underneath, my own harmless, mundane, and dutiful self.

There was a full moon, I think; there ought to have been one. The air was crisp; there were fallen leaves; jack-o-lanterns burned on the porches, giving off the exciting odour of singed pumpkin. Everything was as I'd imagined it beforehand, though already I felt it slipping away from me. I was too old, that was the problem. Halloween was for little children. I'd grown beyond it, I was looking down on it from my balloon. Now that I'd arrived at the moment I'd planned for, I couldn't remember why I'd gone to all that trouble.

I was disappointed, too, at the response of the adults who answered the doors. Everyone knew who my friend Annie was portraying – "Raggedy Annie!" they cried with delight, they even got the pun – but to me they said, "And who are you supposed to be?" My cape had a muffling effect, so I often had to repeat the answer twice. "The Headless Horseman." "The headless what?" Then, "What's that you're holding?" they would go on to say. "It's the head. Of the Headless Horseman." "Oh yes, I see." The head would then be admired, though in the overdone way adults had of admiring a thing when they secretly thought it was inept and laughable. It didn't occur to me that if I'd wanted my costume to be understood immediately I should have chosen something more obvious.

However, there was one member of the audience who'd been suitably impressed. It was my little sister, who hadn't yet gone to bed when I'd made my way through the living room en route to the door. She'd taken one look at the shambling black torso and the big boots and the shiny-haired, frowning, bodiless head, and had begun to scream. She'd screamed and screamed, and hadn't been reassured when I'd lifted up the cape to show that it was really only me underneath. If anything, that had made it worse.

Do you remember the head?" I ask my sister. We're in her rackety car, driving over to see our mother, who is now very old, and bedridden, and blind.

My sister doesn't ask, "What head?" She knows what head. "It looked like a pimp," she says. "With that greaser hair." Then she says, "Smart move, Fred." She talks out loud to other, inferior drivers when she's driving, a thing she does adroitly. All of the other drivers are named Fred, even the women.

THE HEADLESS HORSEMAN

"How do you know what a pimp looks like?"

"You know what I mean."

"A dead pimp, then," I say.

"Not completely dead. The eyes followed you around the room like those 3-D Jesuses."

"They couldn't have. They were sort of crossed."

"They did, though. I was afraid of it."

"You played with it, later," I say. "When you were older. You used to make it talk."

"I was afraid of it anyway," she says. "That's right, Fred, take the whole road."

"Maybe I warped you in childhood," I say.

"Something did," she says, and laughs.

For a while after that Halloween, the head lived in the trunk room, which contained not only two steamer trunks filled with things of my mother's from her previous life — tea cloths she'd embroidered for her trousseau, long kid gloves she'd saved — but also a number of empty suitcases, and the metal box of fly-tying equipment, and the archery materials, and an assortment of miscellaneous items I used to rummage through and pilfer. The head was on an upper shelf, the one with the battered skates and the leather boots — my father's, also my mother's. Foot, foot, foot, foot, head, foot, foot, foot — if you weren't ready for this arrangement and happened to glance up at it, the effect could be disconcerting.

By that time we had a second phone in the house so I could talk with my boyfriends, or go through what passed for talking, without exasperating my father too much — he thought phone conversations should be short, and should convey information. The door to the trunk room was right beside the phone. I liked to keep that door closed while I was talking; otherwise I could see the head staring out at me through the gloom, blood dribbling from the corner of its mouth. With its sleek black hair and minimal chin, it looked like a comic-book head waiter who'd got into a fight. At the same time it seemed malignantly attentive, as if it was taking in every word I said and putting a sour construction on my motives.

After its period of retreat in the trunk room, the head migrated into my sister's dress-up box. By now, I was fifteen and my sister was four. She was still an anxious child – if anything, she was more anxious than ever. She didn't sleep through the night – she'd wake up five or six or seven or nine or ten or eleven times, according to my mother. Although I had the room right next to hers, I never heard her plaintive calls and frightened wailing. I slept through it all as if drugged.

But sleeping mothers hear the cries of their own children, we've been told. They can't help it. Studies have been done. My mother was no exception: she'd hear the little voice calling to her across the blankness of sleep, she'd half wake, then stumble into my sister's room, soothe her mechanically, bring her drinks of water, tuck her in again, then go back to bed and fall asleep, only to be wakened once more and then once more and then once more. She'd grown thinner and thinner in the last four years, her skin pale, her hair brittle and greying, her eyes unnaturally large.

In actuality, she'd caught a disease of the thyroid from the hamster we'd foisted on my sister as a pet in the vain hope that the sound of it creaking round and around on its exercise wheel at night would be calming to her. It was this disease that accounted for my mother's scrawniness and staring eyes: once diagnosed, it was easily cured. But that detail tended to get sidelined during the later

THE HEADLESS HORSEMAN

recountings of this story, both by my mother and by me. The fairy child, the changeling who didn't follow the convenient patterns of other children, who sucked up its mother's energy in an uncanny and nocturnal manner — this is a theme with more inherent interest to it than a hamster-transmitted thyroid disease.

My sister did look a little like a fairy changeling. She was tiny, with blond braids and big blue eyes, and a rabbity way of nibbling on her lower lip as if to keep it from trembling. Her approach to life was tentative. New foods made her nervous, new people, new experiences: she stood at the edge of them, extended a finger, touched gingerly, then more often than not turned away. *No* was a word she learned early. At children's parties she was reluctant to join in the games; birthday cake made her throw up. She was particularly apprehensive about doors, and about who might come through them.

Thus it was probably a bad idea of my father's to pretend to be a bear, a game that had been a great success with his two older children. My sister was fascinated by this game as well, but her interest took a different form. She didn't understand that the bear game was supposed to be fun — that it was an excuse for laughing, shrieking, and running away. Instead, she wanted to observe the bear without being spotted by it herself. This was the reason she'd snipped two holes at eye level in my mother's floor-to-ceiling drapes. She'd go in behind the drapes and peek out through the holes, waiting in a state of paralyzed terror for my father to come home. Would he be a bear, or would he be a father? And even if he looked like a father, would he turn into a bear without warning? She could never be sure.

My mother was not delighted when she discovered the holes cut in her drapes. They were lined drapes; my mother had pleated and hemmed them herself, not because she liked sewing but because it was a good deal cheaper that way. But there was nothing to be done. With a child like that, punishment was beside the point: the poor little thing was in a constant state of suffering anyway, over one thing or another. Her reactions were always in excess of the occasion for them. What was to be done? What was to be done, in particular, about the waking up at night? Surely it wasn't normal. My sister was carted off to see the doctor, who was no help. "She'll grow out of it," was all he would say. He didn't say when.

Because of her sensitivity, or perhaps because my mother was so worn down, my sister was allowed to get away with things I would never have been allowed to do, or so I felt. She spent most meal-times underneath the table instead of on a chair drawn up to it, and while down there she tied people's shoelaces together.

Remember the shoelace thing?" I say to her. "We never knew exactly why you did that."

"I hated sitting at the dinner table," she says. "It was so boring for me. I didn't really have a brother and a sister. I was more like an only child, except with two mothers and two fathers. Two and two, and then me."

"But why the shoelaces?"

"Who knows? Maybe it was a joke."

"You weren't very joke-prone at that age."

"I wanted the two of you to like me. I wanted to be funny."

"You are funny! We do like you!"

"I know, but that was then. You didn't pay much attention to me. You always talked about grown-up things."

"That's hardly fair," I say. "I spent a lot of time with you."

"You had to," she says. "They made you do it."

"They had this idea that I was good with you," I say. "That's what they used to say: 'You're always so good with her.'"

"Way to go, Fred, you moron!" says my sister. "Did you see that? Nobody ever signals. Yeah, well, it let them off the hook."

"I made you those moss gardens," I say defensively. These had been a special thing for her: I put them together in the sandbox, with moss for the trees and bushes, picket fences made of sticks, wet sand houses trimmed with pebbles. Paths paved with flower petals. She'd watch, enraptured: her face would brighten, she'd become very quiet, as if listening. The real garden had that effect on her too. It was at its height then. She'd stand among the irises and poppies, stock-still, as if enchanted. "Moss gardens," I say. "And gardens with little shells in them – you loved them. I made those too."

"Not at the dinner table, though," she says. "It's okay, the light's green, you can go! And then after dinner you used to shut me out of your room."

"I had to study. I couldn't play with you all the time."

"You just didn't want me messing up your stuff. Anyway you weren't always studying. You were reading Perry Mason books and trying on lipstick. And then you left, when I was eight. You abandoned me."

"Nine," I say. "I didn't *abandon* you. I was twenty-one! I left home and got a job. That's what people do."

"It's no left turn before six, Fred, you creep! I wish I had a camera. The thing is," says my sister, "I couldn't figure out who you were supposed to *be*."

My sister had a friend who was a lot like her – another quiet, shy, anxious, big-eyed fairy child, dark where my sister was fair, but with

33

the same china fragility. Leonie was her name. They both insisted on wearing flouncy skirts instead of jeans, they both chose *The Twelve Dancing Princesses* as their favourite story. They longed to have me doll them up in outfits improvised from the dress-up box: I'd pin up their hair and put lipstick on them and let them wear my clip-on earrings. Then they'd prance around solemnly in my high-heeled shoes, holding up their too-long play skirts, keeping their red mouths prim.

"Remember the cut velvet?" my sister says. We're in her car again, going to see our mother again. We prefer to do it together. The rundown house with its flaking paint, the tangle of weeds that used to be the garden, our shrivelled mother — we can deal with these better together. We both have soggy raisin-studded muffins in paper bags and takeout coffees in evil Styrofoam cups: we buy ourselves snacks and bribes, we need to be bolstered up.

"She should never have let us have that," I say. "She should have saved it."

The cut velvet was an evening gown, black, white, and silver in colour, dating from the 1930s. Why had our mother given it to us? Why had she cast away such a treasure, as if abdicating from her former life — her life as a young woman who'd enjoyed herself and had adventures? We'd each admired this gown in turn; we'd each ruined it in the course of our admiration.

"*We* wouldn't have done that," I say. "Wasted it."

"No. We wouldn't. We'd have been selfish. Just throw the garbage in the back seat, I keep it strewn with trash back there to deter burglars."

"I wouldn't call it selfish, as such," I say.

"Not that they'd want to steal this rust bucket. Hoarding, then. We're going to be those old ladies they find in houses full of stacks of newspapers and pickle jars and cat-food tins."

THE HEADLESS HORSEMAN

"I'm not. I have no interest in the cat-food tins."

"Old age is the pits," says my sister. "I kept a piece of it."

"You did?"

"And that skirt of yours with the big red roses – I kept some of that. And a bit of your blue brocade formal. I thought it was so glamorous! I thought everything you did was glamorous. Fred, you asshole! Did you see how she cut me off?"

"What about the pink tulle?"

"I think Mum used it for dusters."

"No great loss," I say. "It looked like a cake."

"I thought it was great – I was going to have one just like it when I grew up. But by the time I got to high school, no one went to formal dances any more."

My sister and Leonie played decorous games together in which life was agreeable, people were gentle and fastidious, and time was divided into predictable routines. They adored miniatures: tiny glass vases with midget flowers in them, eensy-teensy cups and spoons, minute boxes – anything small and dainty. Stuffed-bunny tea parties and doll-dressing absorbed them. All the stranger, then, that they found the Headless Horseman's head in the trunk room, and got it down from the boot shelf, and adopted it.

There it would be, eyes crossed, mouth drooling blood, set in its place between the flop-eared white bunny and the rubber-skinned Sparkle Plenty doll that had led a far riskier and more disreputable life when it had been mine. The head looked out of place but comfortable: everything was done to make it feel at home. A table napkin would be tucked around its neck stump, and it would be served cups of water tea and imaginary cookies just as if it had a body. Better still, it answered when spoken to – it said, "Thank you very much" and "Could I have another cookie, please" and replied to the white bunny and the Sparkle Plenty doll when they asked it if it was having a good time. Sometimes it was made to nod. When the party had been too tiring for it, it was put to sleep in the dolls' bed, with a crocheted quilt pulled up over its receding chin.

Once, I discovered it propped up on my sister's pillow, its neck wrapped in one of our mother's best linen dishtowels. Cookie fragments on dolls' plates were laid out around it, mixed with berries from the prickly-berry hedge, like offerings made to appease an idol. It was wearing a chaplet woven of carrot fronds and marigolds that my sister and Leonie had picked in the garden. The flowers were wilted, the garland was lopsided; the effect was astonishingly depraved, as if a debauched Roman emperor had arrived on the scene and had hacked off his own body in a maiden's chamber as the ultimate sexual thrill.

"Why do you like it so much?" I asked my sister and Leonie. I still took some interest in the head: it was, after all, my creature, though I'd been so young – it seemed to me now – when I'd made it. I regarded it critically: the thing was really unconvincing. The nose and chin were way too small, the skull too square, the hair too black. I should have done a better job.

They gazed up at me with distrust. "We don't *like* him," said my sister.

"We're taking care of him," said Leonie.

"He's sick," said my sister. "We're the nurses."

"We're making him feel better," said Leonie.

"Does he have a name?" I asked.

The two little girls looked at each other. "His name is Bob," said Leonie.

This struck me as funny. I tried not to laugh: my sister was affronted when I laughed at anything to do with her. "Bob the Head?" I said. "That's his name?"

"You're not supposed to laugh at him," said my sister in an injured tone.

"Why not?" I said.

"Because it's not his fault," she said.

"What's not?"

"That he's got no, got no . . ."

"Got no body?" I said.

"Yes," said my sister in a stricken voice. "It's not his fault! It's only the way he is!" By this time the tears were trickling down her cheeks.

Leonie gave me an indignant stare; she picked up the head and hugged it. "You shouldn't be so mean," she told me.

"I know," I said. "You're right. I shouldn't be so mean." But I had to go into my room and close the door, because I had to either laugh or choke.

Yet at other times the two of them demanded meanness from me. They'd pester me ceaselessly because they wanted me to play a game called Monster. I was supposed to be the monster – stalking around the house and out into the yard, legs and arms stiff like a zombie's, calling in a toneless voice, "Where *are* you? Where *are* you?" while they held hands and ran away from me, and hid behind the shrubs or the furniture, twittering with fright. When I got home from school they'd be waiting; they'd turn their delicate little pansy-eyed faces up to me and plead, "Be a monster! Be a monster!" Their appetite for my monstrousness was boundless; as long as the two of them were together, holding hands, they could tough it out, they could escape, they could defy me.

Sometimes my sister would be alone when I got home. By "alone," I mean without Leonie, for of course my mother would be there. Not for long, however: she'd grab the opening provided by my arrival and be off like a shot, heading for the grocery store or some other equally spurious destination, leaving me as impromptu babysitter. Really she wanted the open road; she wanted speed and exercise, and her own thoughts. She wanted to be free of us – all of us – if only for an hour. But I didn't recognize that then.

"Okay," I'd say. "I have to do my homework. You can play over there. Why don't you have a dolly tea party?" But no sooner would I have settled myself with my books than my sister would start up.

"Be a monster! Be a monster!" she would say.

"I don't think it's a good idea. Leonie isn't here. You'll cry."

"No, I won't."

"Yes, you will. You always do."

"I won't this time. Please! Please!"

"All right," I'd say, though I was quite sure how it would end. "I'll count to ten. Then I'm coming to get you." I said this last in my flat monster voice. By the time I'd reached ten, my sister would already have shut herself into the front hall closet with the winter coats and the vacuum cleaner, and would be calling in a muffled voice, "The game's over! The game's over!"

"All right," I would say in a reasonable but still eerie tone. "The game's over. You can come out now."

"No! You're still being a monster!"

"I'm not a monster. I'm only your sister. It's safe to come out."

THE HEADLESS HORSEMAN

"Stop it! Stop it! Stop the game!"

"Stop what? There isn't any game."

"Stop it! Stop it!"

I shouldn't have done that. A sister pretending to be a monster, or a monster pretending to be a sister? It was too much for her to decipher. Small children have trouble with ill-defined borders, and my sister had more trouble than most. I knew perfectly well, even while I was speaking in my duplicitous voice, what the results would be: sobbing and hysteria and then, many hours later, nightmares. In the middle of the night, screams of terror would issue from my sister's bedroom; my mother would be dragged from unconsciousness, hoisting herself grimly out of bed, shuffling across the hall to mollify and soothe, while I slept through it all, conked out like a slug drowning in beer, evading the fallout from my crimes.

"What did you do to her?" my mother would say when she got back from her shopping excursion. My sister would still be in the front hall closet, weeping, afraid to come out. I'd be sitting at the dining-room table, placidly doing my homework.

"Nothing. We were playing Monster. She wanted to."

"You know how impressionable she is."

I'd shrug and smile. I could scarcely be blamed for being obliging.

Why did I behave this way? I didn't know. My excuse – even, on some level, to myself – was that I was simply giving in to an urgent demand, a demand made by my little sister. I was humouring her. I was indulging her. Of more interest to me now is why my sister made the demand, again and again. Did she believe she'd finally be able to face down my monster self, deal with it on her own terms? Did she hope that I would finally – at last – transform myself, on cue, into who I was really supposed to be?

. . .

Why did you like the monster game?" I say to her.

"I don't know," she says. "Drop dead, Fred, the light was red. Do you want lunch before Mum, or after?"

"If we have it before, we'll get depressed with no treat to look forward to. On the other hand I'm starving."

"So am I. Let's go to Satay on the Road."

"Or we could go to Small Talk. They have good soup."

"I make a lot of soup at home. I need some of that peanut sauce. Should I dye my hair red? I'm getting a lot of grey."

"It looks good," I say. "It looks distinguished."

"But what about red?"

"Why not?" I say. "If you like. I could never handle red, but you can."

"It's bizarre, because we're both yellow/orange, according to the colour charts."

"I know. You can do lime green too. It makes me look bloodless. You used to agitate and agitate for that monster game and then shut yourself up in the front hall closet as soon as it began."

"I remember that. I remember that feeling of being completely terrified. Warm wool, vacuum cleaner smell, terror."

"But you kept on wanting to do it. Did you think you could make it come out differently?"

"It's like saying, 'Tomorrow morning I'm going to get up early and work out.' And then the time comes and you just can't."

"Mother used to think it was her fault," I say.

"What, me hiding in the coat closet?"

"Oh . . . and other stuff," I say. "The whole picture. Remember when you were going through that total honesty period?"

"I've stopped?"

"Well, no. I never went in for it, myself – total honesty. I preferred lying."

"Oh, you never lied much."

I duck that one. "Anyway, you were halfway through high school when you really got going on the honesty. You were going to tell Mum and Dad about drugs, and skipping school, and kids your age having sex, because you thought Mum and Dad led a protected life and were too repressed."

"Well, they did and they were," she says. "I did tell them about some of it. I told them about taking LSD."

"What did they say?"

"Dad pretended he hadn't heard. Mum said, 'What was it like?'"

"I didn't know you took LSD."

"I only took it once," she says. "It wasn't that great. It was like a really long car trip. I kept wondering when it would end."

"That's what happened to me too," I say.

When my sister was sixteen and I was twenty-eight, my parents called me home. This had never happened before: it was in the nature of an SOS. They were becoming increasingly desperate: my sister had added anger to her repertoire of emotions. She still cried a lot, but she cried from fury as well as from despair. Or she'd go into thick, silent rages that were like a dense black fog descending over everyone. I'd witnessed these at family Christmas dinners – events I now tried to avoid as much as possible.

My parents persisted in their belief that I was particularly good with my sister – better than my brother, who did not take emotional outbursts seriously. They themselves certainly weren't good with her, my mother told me. They wanted her to be happy – she was so bright, she had such potential – but she was so immature. They just didn't know what to do. "Maybe we were too old to have another child," my mother said. "We don't understand these things. When I was that age, if you were unhappy you kept it to yourself."

"She's a teenager," I said. "They're all like that. It's hormones."

"You weren't like that when you were a teenager," said my mother hopefully.

"I was more furtive," I said. I didn't go on to say that she could hardly have any idea of what I'd been like then because she'd been in a coma most of the time. I'd done a lot of things she'd known nothing about, but I wasn't going to reveal them now. "She's right out in the open," I said.

"She certainly is," said my mother.

My parents had wanted me to come home because they had a chance to go to Europe – it was some sort of group trip, it wouldn't cost much – and they had never been there. They wanted to see castles. They wanted to see Scotland, and the Eiffel Tower. They were like excited kids. But they were afraid to leave my sister on her own: she took things too hard, and she was going through a bad period. ("Over some boy," said my mother, with slight contempt. As a young woman she'd have let herself be boiled in oil before admitting to a bad period over some boy. The thing then was to have lots of beaus, and to treat them all with smiling disdain.)

They'd only be gone for two weeks, said my father. A little more than that, said my mother, with a mixture of guilt and anxiety. Eighteen days. Twenty, counting the travel.

I didn't see how I could deny them. They were getting old, or what I thought of as old. They were almost sixty. They might never have another chance to see a castle. So I said yes.

THE HEADLESS HORSEMAN

It was the summer — a Toronto summer, hot and humid. My parents had never bothered with air conditioning or fans — physical discomfort didn't mean much to them — so the house got progressively warmer as the day advanced, and didn't cool off until midnight. By this time my sister was living in my former bedroom, so I found myself in hers.

Our days fell into a strange pattern, or lack of pattern. We got up when we felt like it and went to bed at irregular hours. We ate our meals here and there around the house, and let the dirty dishes pile up on the kitchen counter before doing them. Sometimes we took our lunches down to the cellar, where it was cooler. We read detective stories and bought women's magazines, which we leafed through in order to rearrange ourselves, though only in theory. I was too tired to do much of anything else; or not tired, sleepy. I'd fall asleep on the chesterfield in the middle of the day, sink down into cavernous dreams, then wake up groggily toward suppertime, feeling hungover. Ordinarily I never took naps.

Once in a while we'd make forays into the blazing-hot garden, to water it according to the meticulous instructions left by our parents — instructions we did not follow — or to yank out the more blatant weeds, the deadly nightshade vines, the burdocks, the sow thistles; or to snip fragments off the exuberant prickly-berry hedge, which was threatening to take over the entire side border. The phlox was in bloom, the dahlias, the zinnias: the colours were dizzying. We made an effort at mowing the lawn with the elderly push mower that had been around forever. We'd left it too long: the mower blades got clogged with crushed grass and clover.

"Maybe it's time they entered the twentieth century and got a gas mower," I said.

"I think we should mow the whole garden," said my sister. "Flatten it right out."

"Then it would all be lawn. More to mow. Let's anyway trim the edges."

"Why bother? It's too much effort. I'm thirsty."

"Okay. So am I." And we'd go inside.

At unpredictable moments, I heard many instalments about a boy called Dave, who played the drums and was unobtainable. It was always the same story: my sister loved Dave, Dave didn't love her. Maybe he'd loved her once, or had begun to, but then something had happened. She didn't know what. Her life was ruined. She could never possibly ever be happy again. Nobody loved her.

"He sounds like a drip," I said.

"He's not a drip! It was so great once!"

"I'm just going by what you told me. I didn't hear about any great parts. Anyway, if he's not interested, he's not interested."

"You're always so fucking logical!" My sister had taken up swearing at a much earlier age than I had, and was fluent in it.

"I'm not, really," I said. "I just don't know what I'm supposed to say."

"You used everything up. You used up all the good parts," said my sister. "There was nothing left over for me."

This was deep water. "What do you mean?" I said carefully. "What exactly did I use up?"

My sister was wiping tears from her eyes. She had to think a little, pick something out from the overflowing pool of sadness. "Dancing," she said. "You used up dancing."

"You can't use up dancing," I said. "Dancing is something you *do*. You can *do* whatever you want."

"No, I can't."

"Yes, you really can. It's not me stopping you."

"Maybe I shouldn't be on this planet," said my sister grimly. "Maybe I should never have been born."

I felt as if I were groping through brambles in a night so dark I couldn't see my own hands. *At my wit's end* had been, before this, merely an expression, but now it described a concrete reality: I could see my wits unrolling like a ball of string, length after length of wits being played out, each length failing to hold fast, breaking off as if rotten, until finally the end of the string would be reached, and what then? How many days were left for me to fill – for me to fill responsibly – before the real parents would come back and take over, and I could escape to my life?

Maybe they would never come back. Maybe I would have to stay here forever. Maybe both of us would have to stay here forever, trapped in our present ages, never getting any older, while the garden grew up like a forest and the prickly-berry bush swelled to the size of a tree, blotting the light from the windows.

In a state of near-panic I suggested to my sister that we should go on an excursion. An adventure. We would go to the town of Kitchener, on the Greyhound bus. It was only about an hour. Kitchener had some lovely old houses in it; we would take pictures of them with my camera. I'd been taking a lot of pictures of architecture around that time – nineteenth-century Ontario buildings. It was an interest of mine, I said, not lying very much. Oddly enough, my sister agreed to this plan. I'd been expecting her to refuse it: too complicated, too much effort, why bother?

We set off the next day supplied with oranges and digestive biscuits, and made it to the bus station without incident, and sat through the bus trip in relative calm. Then we ambled around in Kitchener, looking at things. I took pictures of houses. We bought sandwiches. We went to the park and watched the swans.

While we were in the park, an older woman said to us, "Are you twins?"

"Yes," said my sister. "We are!" Then she laughed and said, "No, we're not. We're only sisters."

"Well, you look like twins," said the woman.

We were the same height. We had the same noses. We were wearing similar clothes. I could see how the woman might have thought that, supposing she was a little nearsighted. The idea alarmed me: before that moment, I'd viewed the two of us in terms of our differences. Now I saw that we were more alike than I'd imagined. I had more layers on, more layers of gauze; that was all.

My sister's mood had changed. Now she was almost euphoric. "Look at the swans," she said. "They're so, they're so . . ."

"Swanlike," I said. I felt almost giddy. The afternoon sun was golden on the pond where the swans floated; a mellow haze suffused the air. Suffused, I thought. That was how I felt. Maybe our parents were right: perhaps I alone had the magic key, the one that would open the locked door and free my sister from the dungeon that appeared to be enclosing her.

"It was great to come here," she said. Her face was radiant.

But the next day she was more unhappy than ever. And after that it got worse. Whatever magic I thought I might have – or that everyone thought I might have – proved useless. The good times became fewer, the bad times worse. They became worse and worse, for years and years. Nobody knew why.

My sister sits on the bottom step of my stairs, biting her fingers and crying. This doesn't happen once, but many times. "I should just

THE HEADLESS HORSEMAN

leave," she says. "I should just check out. I'm useless here. It's too much effort." She means: *getting through time*.

"You've had fun," I say. "Haven't you? There's lots of things you like."

"That was a while ago," she says. "It's not enough. I'm tired of playing the game. This is the wrong place for me to be."

She doesn't mean my house. She means her body. She means the planet Earth. I can see the same thing she's seeing: it's a cliff edge, it's a bridge with a steep drop, it's the end. That's what she's wants: *The End*. Like the end of a story.

"You aren't useless, you shouldn't leave!" I say. "You'll feel better tomorrow!" But it's like calling across a wide field to a person on the other side. She can't hear me. Already she's turning away, looking down, looking down over, preparing for dark flight.

She'll be lost. I will lose her. I'm not close enough to stop her.

"That would be a terrible thing to do," I say.

"There's no other door," she says. "Don't worry. You're really strong. You'll handle it."

We turn a corner and then another, pass a willow tree and then a weeping mulberry, pull into the driveway of our mother's house. "Look at Fred," says my sister. "Parked right in the middle of the street. If I was a snowplow, I'd plow him right into the prickly-berry hedge."

"That's the spirit," I say. We clamber out of the car, which is getting harder for me to do. Something happens to the knees. I stand, one hand on the car, stretching myself, surveying the ruined garden. "I need to tackle that yew tree," I say. "I forgot my pruners. There's deadly nightshade vine all through it."

"Why bother?" says my sister in full honesty mode. "Mum can't see it."

"I can," I say. "Other people can. She used to be so proud of that garden."

"You worry too much about other people. Was I a really horrible child?"

"Not at all," I say. "You were very cute. You had big blue eyes and little blond braids."

"According to the stories I whined a lot."

"It wasn't whining," I say. "You had a sensitive nervous system. You had an enhanced reaction to reality."

"In other words, I whined a lot."

"You wanted the world to be better than it was," I say.

"No, that was you. You wanted that. I just wanted it to be better than it was for *me*."

I sidestep that. "You were very affectionate," I say. "You appreciated things. You appreciated them more than other people. You practically went into trances of rapture."

"But I'm all right now," she says. "Thank God for pharmaceuticals."

"Yes," I say. "You're all right now."

She takes a pill every day, for a chemical imbalance she was born with. That was it, all along. That was what made the bad times for her. Not my monstrousness at all.

I believe that, most of the time.

Now we're at the door. The persistence of material objects is becoming an amazement to me. It's the same door – the one I used to go in through, out through, year after year, in my daily clothing or in various outfits and disguises, not thinking at all that I would one day be standing in front of this very same door with my grey-haired little sister. But all doors used regularly are doors to the afterlife.

"I lost track of that head," I say. "The Headless Horseman head. Remember when it lived in the trunk room? Remember all those boots, and the archery supplies?"

"Vaguely," says my sister.

"We'll have to go through that stuff, you know. When the time comes. We'll have to sort it out."

"I'm not looking forward to it," says my sister.

"Where did it go, in the end? That head? Did you get rid of it?"

"Oh, it's still down there somewhere," says my sister.

My Last Duchess

T hat's my last Duchess painted on the wall,'" said Miss Bessie. No one would have called her *Miss Bessie* to her face, but that was her name among us. It was far more respectful than our names for some of the other teachers: the Gorilla, the Crip, the Hippo. "Now, class. What does that single word, *last*, tell us right away?"

The windows of our brand-new schoolroom were high enough so we couldn't see anything out of them except the sky. Today the sky was a hazy blue, a warm, drowsy colour. I wasn't looking at it, but there it was, at the edge of eyesight, huge and featureless and soothing, rolling on and on like the sea. One of the window panels was open and some flies had come in. They were buzzing around, bumbling against the glass, trying to get out. I could hear them, but I couldn't see them, I couldn't risk turning my head. I was supposed to be thinking about *last*.

Last, last, last. Last was so close to *lost.* Last Duchess. *Duchess* was an insinuating rustle, a whispering: taffeta brushing over a floor. On a day like this it was hard to resist dozing off, drifting down into reverie or half-sleep. It was afternoon, it was May, the trees outside were flowering, pollen was eddying everywhere. The classroom was too hot; it was filled with a vibration, the vibration of its newness – the blond wood of its curved, modern metal-framed desks, the greenness of its blackboards, the faint humming of its fluorescent lights, which seemed to hum even when they were turned off. But despite this newness there was an old smell in the room, an ancient, fermenting smell: an invisible steam was rising all around, oily, salty, given off by twenty-five adolescent bodies stewing gently in the humid springtime air.

Last Duchess. There had to be more than one, then. A whole bunch of Duchesses, all in a row like a chorus line. No: it was *last* as in *last year.* The Duchess was back there in the past – gone, over with, left behind.

Quite frequently Miss Bessie didn't wait for anyone to stick up a hand: it could be a long wait, as being too quick to blurt stuff out was ridiculous in our eyes. We didn't want to make fools of ourselves by getting a thing wrong, or else – sometimes equally foolish – by getting it right. Miss Bessie was well aware of that, so nine times out of ten she simply answered her own questions. "*Last* Duchess tells us," she said, "that this Duchess is no longer the wife of the Duke. It also implies that there may be a *next* Duchess. The first line of a poem is very important, class. It sets the tone. Let us proceed."

Miss Bessie was sitting on top of her desk, as usual. She had good legs, not only for a woman of her age but for any woman, and she wore beautiful shoes – not the kind of shoes we ourselves would have worn, not penny loafers or saddle shoes or velveteen flats or stiletto heels for dancing, but we could tell they were in good taste and well taken care of. No spot or smear of dirt was ever to be seen on those softly gleaming shoes of Miss Bessie's.

Each pair of shoes went with its own outfit, and here too Miss Bessie was exceptional. The female teachers at our school wore tailored suits to do their teaching in. It was a kind of uniform — a skirt, straight or gored or pleated, a matching jacket, a blouse underneath, white or cream-coloured, often with a floppy bow tied at the neckline, and a brooch on the left-hand lapel — but Miss Bessie's suits had an elegance the others could not match. Her blouses were not cheesy, limp nylon but had a sheen and solidity to them, her brooches looked as if their semi-precious stones were real: her best one was amber and gold, in the shape of a bee. Her hair wasn't grey but silver, and expertly waved; her cheekbones were prominent, her jaw firm, her eyes piercing; her nose, discreetly powdered, was *aquiline*, a word we had learned from her.

We pitied the other female teachers in our school — hopeless, ill-groomed drudges, overwrought and easily distracted, shackled to a thankless task, namely teaching us — but we did not pity Miss Bessie.

It wasn't only her no-nonsense professional appearance the boys in the class respected: it was the fact that she had an M.A. Those two letters were a qualification: they stood for something important, like M.D. So the boys respected that, but they also respected the tight leash on which she kept them. "Richard, do you have something amusing to say? If so, be so kind as to say it to all of us." "David, that observation is beneath you. You can do better than that. A man's reach should exceed his grasp." "Robert, was that a flimsy attempt at wit?" *Sarcastic* was the word we used, about such remarks. But Miss

Bessie was never sarcastic about honest blunders. She was patient with those.

"Now then. 'That's my last Duchess painted on the wall,'" said Miss Bessie, "'Looking as if she were alive.' *As if* she were alive. Class, what does *as if* tell us?"

This time she did wait. I never knew – none of us knew – when one of her waits would set in. They always woke me up. It was the suspense, the looming danger – the threat of being pounced on, called by name, forced to speak. At such times my mouth would fill with words, too many of them, a glutinous pudding of syllables I would have to mould into speech while Miss Bessie's ironic narrowed eyes beamed their message at me: *You can do better than that.* During such waiting periods I found it best to look down – otherwise Miss Bessie might single me out – and so I busied myself by making notes in my notebook.

He bumped her off, I wrote. *Bumped her off* was not a thing I would ever have said out loud in class, as it was slang and Miss Bessie disapproved of such sloppy and vulgar talk. I'd picked up *bumped off* from the detective stories I was in the habit of reading as a way of evading my homework, or at least delaying it. Unfortunately, there were a lot of detective stories in the house, along with historical novels and books about World War One, and about monasteries in Tibet – a country where women could have two husbands at the same time – and about naval warfare in Napoleonic times, and about the form and function of the Fallopian tubes. If I wasn't in the mood for a whole book, I'd go through the stacks of old *Life*s and *Times* and *Chatelaine*s and *Good Housekeeping*s – my parents were reluctant to throw anything out – and puzzle over the ads (what was a douche?) and the articles on fashion and personal problems (*Teenage Rebellion: Five Antidotes. Halitosis: Your Silent Enemy. Can This Marriage Be Saved?*).

I'd learned quite a lot, over the years, by avoiding what I was supposed to be learning.

Bumped off, I wrote. The Duke had bumped off the Duchess. Cheap floozies often got bumped off, and so did hot tomatoes and dumb bunnies, and so did sleazy broads. *Bumped* suggested a blow to the head with a blunt instrument, such as a blackjack, but this was not likely the method the Duke had used on the Duchess. Nor had he buried her in the cellar and covered up the grave with wet cement, or cut her up into pieces and heaved the pieces into the lake or dropped them down a well or left them in a park, like the husbands in some of the more grisly narratives I'd encountered. I thought he'd most likely poisoned her: it was a well-known fact among the writers of historical romances that Dukes of that time were expert poisoners. They had rings with hollow stones on the fronts and they slid the stones open when nobody was looking and slipped the poison into people's flagons of wine, in powder form. Arsenic was a substance they favoured. The poor Duchess would have sickened gradually; a doctor would have been called in, a sinister doctor in the pay of the Duke. This doctor would have mixed up a final, lethal, potion to finish her off. There would have been a touching death scene and then a fancy funeral, with candles, and after that the Duke would have been free to go on the prowl for another beautiful girl to turn into a Duchess and then bump off.

On second thought, I decided that the Duke wouldn't have lifted a finger in the matter himself: he was far too snobbish to have bothered with any of the actual poisoning. *I gave commands*, he said, later on in the poem. (I'd skipped ahead.) The dirty work would have been done by some thug with a name like First Murderer – as in plays by Shakespeare – while the Duke himself was elsewhere, dropping names and paying phony compliments and showing off his costly artworks. I had a picture of how he would look: he'd be dark and suave and insultingly polite, and would wear a lot of velvet. There were movie stars like that, such as James Mason. They always had classy English accents. The Duke would have had an accent like that, even though he was Italian.

"Well?" said Miss Bessie. "The subject is *as if*. We don't have all day. Marilyn?"

"Maybe she's dead," said Marilyn.

"Very good, Marilyn," said Miss Bessie. "That is one possibility. The attentive reader, I said *attentive*, Bill, this does apply to you, unless you have some other more important engagement to attend to — no? — the *attentive* reader would certainly wonder that, and might wonder also — *if* the Duchess is indeed dead — how she might have died."

At the sound of Bill's name I found myself blushing, because Bill was my boyfriend; to be on the receiving end of Miss Bessie's sarcasm was humiliating for him, and therefore by extension for me. It was true that Bill was not an attentive reader, but he regretted it, or else he resented it, I wasn't sure which. I could visualize him now, two rows behind me, going red in the face with shame and anger as his friends smirked at him. But Miss Bessie didn't care about that. She trampled right over you if she thought you were fooling around — if you got in the way of her teaching.

"Of course we often say of a portrait, 'It's very lifelike,'" she continued. "That would be the other possibility. Perhaps this remark of the Duke's is merely a comment on the verisimilitude — the *lifelikeness* — of the portrait itself. The entire poem is told from the Duke's point of view — therefore nothing he says may be taken as objective truth. We will return to this question of *point of view* later."

Verisimilitude, I wrote in my notebook. *Lifelike. The Duchess is almost alive. Point of view.*

Miss Bessie was the best English teacher in the school. Possibly she was one of the best in the city: our parents said we were lucky to have her. She drove us briskly through the curriculum as if herding sheep, heading us off from false detours and perilous cliff edges, nipping at our heels when we slowed down in the wrong places, making us linger in the right ones so we could assimilate the material of importance. She described our task of learning as a race, a sort of obstacle course: there was a lot of ground still to be covered before the final exams, she said, and it had to be covered rapidly. This ground was strewn with hurdles and rough parts, and other difficulties. The days were speeding by, and we still had *Tess of the d'Urbervilles* looming up ahead of us like – we felt – a big steep hill of mud. It was true that once we got to the top of it, Miss Bessie – who'd been up there many times before – might show us a view; but meanwhile there would be a lot of slipperiness. We'd tangled with Thomas Hardy in the form of *The Mayor of Casterbridge* the year before: it was going to be heavy slogging. Therefore we needed to polish off the Last Duchess before week's end so we could catch our breath over the weekend and then get a good run at *Tess*.

> "That's my last Duchess painted on the wall,
> Looking as if she were alive. I call
> That piece a wonder, now; Frà Pandolf's hands
> Worked busily a day, and there she stands.
> Will't please you sit and look at her?"

"Now, class. 'Will't please *you*.' To whom do you suppose the Duke is speaking?"

Line by line, Miss Bessie hauled us through the poem. It was an important poem, worth — said Miss Bessie — a full fifteen marks on the final exam. English was a compulsory subject: we couldn't get out of high school without passing it. But Miss Bessie wasn't interested in mere passes; she wanted top marks from us. She had the reputation of the school to keep up, and also her own reputation. Her students did well because they were well prepared. "You must be *well prepared*," she told us frequently. "Of course, you will have covered the material, but in addition to that you must read the question twice and make sure you answer what is being asked. You must keep your head and not panic. You must *outline* and *structure*." For each piece of work we studied, she produced a sampling of the questions that had been asked in previous years and drilled us in the acceptable answers.

Once we had written them, the exams would be centrally marked by a hand-picked team of markers, and then, one day in August, the final grades would be published in the newspaper, brutally, without warning, to be seen by everyone — our friends, our enemies, our families. We dreaded this. It would be like having someone yank open the curtain when you were taking a shower.

The grades in the newspaper would determine whether we would go on. *Going on* meant going to university. Our school was not for rich kids — they went to private institutions. It didn't matter so much to their lives whether they did well in high school, because a place would be made for them somehow. Neither was it for the poor: we lacked the freedom of being considered too stupid to go on. The dropouts, as we called them, had left as early as they could, but not before they'd tortured us with taunts of "brainer," "brown nose," "show-off," and "suckup," and had jeered relentlessly at anyone who actually did homework. They'd left us with an ambiguous opinion of ourselves. "Think you're so smart," they'd sneered, and we had thought we were smart, smarter than them at any rate; but we didn't altogether approve of our smartness. It was like having an extra hand: an advantage for opening doors, but freakish despite that.

Nonetheless we would have to live by our deformity. We'd have to use our wits, work our way up the ladder provided for us, make something of ourselves. The boys were expected to become doctors, lawyers, dentists, accountants, engineers. As for us girls, we weren't sure where we were headed. If we didn't go on, we'd have to get married, or else become old maids; but with a good set of grades, this dismaying fork in the road could be postponed for a while.

We would sit the exams during a three-week period in June, in the gymnasium. It would be – said Miss Bessie – a turning point in our lives, but if we were well prepared we need not fear this test, which was a test of our characters, not merely of our intelligence. To succeed we would need courage and a steady nerve, and if those qualities were present it would simply be a matter of setting down the right facts and observations in the right order.

Nonetheless we frightened one another with stories about potential disaster. There was no air conditioning in the gym, and if there was a heat wave – as there usually was in June – we would all cook, stew, and fry. Girls had been known to topple out of their desks in a cold faint; other girls had unexpectedly got their periods, and had found themselves sitting in puddles of blood, which – in the more squalid renditions – actually dripped off the seat of the desk onto the floor, plop, plop, plop – a mortifying prospect. Boys had had nervous breakdowns, and had started shouting and swearing;

others had lost their nerve, and everything they'd memorized had vanished right out of their brains, and at the end of the exam it was found they'd been writing nothing but their own names, over and over. One boy had drawn a perfect isosceles triangle on every single page – meticulously, it was emphasized. *Meticulously* was a chilling touch: meticulousness, we knew, was just one step away from full-blown lunacy.

After school I walked home across the football field, a locale that had once been frightening to me, and forbidden, and significant in some way I couldn't define, but which had now shrunk to an irrelevant stretch of muddy grass. A couple of younger kids were having a smoke behind the field house, where sordid orgies involving a girl called Loretta – one of the dropouts – were rumoured to have taken place. I carried my big black leather binder full of notes in front of me, hugging it to my chest with both arms, my textbooks piled on top of it. All the girls did this. It prevented anyone from staring at our breasts, which were either too small and contemptuous, or else too big and hilarious, or else just the right size – but what size was right? Breasts of any kind were shameful and could attract catcalls of "Get a load of the knockers!" from greasy-haired boys lounging in groups, or from young men in cars. Or else they would chant,

> *I must, I must, I must develop my bust!*
> *I better, I better, or I'll never wear a sweater!*

while moving their bent arms back and forth like a cartoon chicken's. Although in truth the catcalling didn't happen very much, there was always the fear that it would. To yell back at the boys was brazen, to ignore them was supposed to be dignified, though it didn't feel dignified, it felt degrading. Merely to have breasts was degrading. But not to have any at all would have been worse.

"Stand up straight, shoulders back, don't slouch," our Physical Education teacher used to bark at us during volleyball practice, centuries ago, in that very same gym where we would soon be writing the finals. But what did she know? She herself was flat-chested, and anyway very old. Forty at least.

Breasts were one thing: they were in front, where you could have some control over them. Then there were bums, which were behind, and out of sight, and thus more lawless. Apart from loosely gathered skirts, nothing much could be done about them.

Hey! Hey! Swing and sway!! Get a load of that wiggle!

Walking beside me across the football field was Bill, who wasn't the sort of boy who would roam around in a pack, shouting things about girls' breasts; or I didn't think he was. He was more serious than that, he had better things to do, he wanted to go places. He wanted to climb the ladder. As my official boyfriend, he walked me partway home every day, except on Fridays when he began his weekend job at a grocery store in the other direction. Fridays after school, Saturdays until three – he was saving the money for university, because his parents couldn't afford it, or wouldn't spare it. Neither of them had gone on and they'd managed fine without. That was their attitude, according to Bill, but he didn't seem to hold it against them.

Several months earlier, Bill had replaced my last boyfriend, who'd replaced the one before that. The process of replacement was delicate – it called for diplomacy, and nuance, and the willpower to resist answering the phone – but at a certain stage it had to be done. That stage came after the earlier, permissible stages had been gone through – the first date, the first tentative holding of hands, the arm around the shoulders in the movie, the slow, gelatinous dancing, the breathy fumbling around in parked cars, the advances and counterattacks of hands, the war of zippers and buttons. After a while, a stalemate would be reached: neither side would know what was supposed to come next. To go forward was unthinkable, to go back impossible. This period was characterized by listlessness, by squabbling and making up, by an inability to decide which movie we wanted to see, and – on my part – by the reading of novels that ended badly, over which I would weep. That was when the boyfriend had to be traded in and a fresh one obtained.

It wasn't that I mourned over the boys individually so much as that I hated to have things finish. I didn't want any phase of my life to be gone forever, to be over and done with. I preferred beginnings to endings in books, as well – it was exciting not to know what was lying in store for me on the unread pages – but, perversely, I couldn't resist sneaking a look at the final chapter of any book I was reading.

As a boyfriend, Bill wasn't following – could not follow – the standard cycle. Behind us were the Saturday-night dates, ahead of us the grim scenario in the gymnasium, with all it might involve: fainting, raving, panic, failure, disgrace. Now that there was so much ground to be covered before June, we no longer had time for the endless evenings parked in a car, with the policemen shining the flashlights in and asking if everything was all right; we no longer had time for the fights, for the sulking, for the monosyllabic phone calls and the grudging forgiveness. Instead of all that, we studied together.

Or, to be accurate, I helped Bill study. What I helped him with was English literature. So far, he'd managed to squeak through it, but now he was frightened, although he didn't call it fright. Instead, he blamed the literature itself: it refused to make sense. He wanted everything to be clear-cut, as in algebra, a subject he was good at. How could there be two or three meanings to one single word at the same time? How could Miss Bessie get all of that stuff out of a single poem? Why couldn't people say things plainly?

Helping Bill wasn't turning out to be easy. He'd get mad at the poem for being complicated; he'd argue with it, and demand that it be different; then he'd get mad at the poet for having written it that way; then he'd get mad at me. After a while he'd say he was sorry, he hadn't meant it – I was really, really smart, in that way at least; I was good with words, not like him, and he admired me for it. He just needed me to explain the thing again, only more slowly. After that we would neck and fumble around, though not for very long because we couldn't afford the time.

This day, Bill and I were in no great hurry to get home. We strolled, we sauntered; we paused for ice cream cones at the drugstore. You had to take a break from the books once in a while, said Bill. The ice cream came in cylinders and tasted faintly of the cardboard in which it had been rolled; the cones themselves were leathery in texture. We reached the funeral parlour and sat down on the low stone wall in front of it. The sunlight was golden; pale greenish tassels dangled from the trees; Bill's hair, which was light brown and cut very short, shone like a soft velvety lawn. It was all I could do to keep from stroking the top of his head, as if he was a plush toy dog, but he wouldn't have liked that. He didn't like to be patted.

"I'm not going to pass it," said Bill. "I'm going to flunk out."

"No, you're not," I said.

"I just don't get it."

"Don't get what?"

"What's going on."

"What's going on in what?" I said, though I knew what he meant.

"That goddamn Duchess poem."

Goddamn was the worst swearing Bill ever did in front of me. To say the other words – the F-word, for instance – would have meant he thought I was the kind of girl you could say such things to. A shoddy girl.

I sighed. "Okay, I'll run over it again. The poem is by Robert Browning. He was one of the most important poets of the nineteenth century. It's a dramatic monologue. That means only one person is speaking, like a monologue in a play. The form is iambic pentameter run-on couplets."

"I get that part," said Bill. Form wasn't difficult for him, because it involved counting. A sonnet, a sestina, an *abab* rhyme-scheme ballad – identifying these caused him no problems.

I finished my ice cream and tucked the end of the cone in between the stone wall and the funeral parlour's flower bed, in which a neat row of red tulips was arranged. I felt lazy, I wasn't really in an instructive mood, but Bill was leaning forward, he was actually listening. "So, it's the Duke of Ferrara speaking," I said. "The whole poem is told from his point of view – that's important, because they always ask about point of view. We know it's Ferrara because it says *Ferrara* right under the title of the poem. Ferrara was a noted centre for the arts in Italy, so it makes sense for the Duke to have a picture collection. The time is the Renaissance. There was a lot of murdering going on then. Okay so far?"

"Yeah, but . . ."

"Okay, so the Duke is talking to an envoy from the Count. We know it's the Count because it says that, right there at the end. He's dickering for the Count's daughter, he wants to get hold of her for his next Duchess. It doesn't say which Count. They're upstairs – the Duke and the envoy. We know that because they come downstairs at the end, where it says, 'Nay, we'll go together down, sir.'"

"Why put that in?" said Bill.

"Put what in?"

"Who cares whether they're upstairs or downstairs?" Bill was already getting exasperated.

"They have to be upstairs because there are other people downstairs – see, look, it's right here – and the Duke wants a private conversation. Anyway, the portrait of the Duchess is upstairs. That's what the Duke is taking the envoy to see. The Duke pulls a curtain. There's the picture of his last Duchess behind it. His *last* Duchess, get it? The picture has verisimilitude."

"What?"

"Verisimilitude. It means *lifelike*. Put that word into your answer on the exam. I bet it's worth a whole mark."

"Cripes," said Bill, giving a rueful little grin. "Sure. If you say so. Okay. Write it down for me."

"Okay. So they stand looking at this Duchess picture. Then basically the Duke tells the envoy about her, and what was wrong with her, and why he bumped her off."

"Or shut her up in a convent," said Bill hopefully. Miss Bessie had proposed this as an alternative, saying that Browning himself had done so. The boys in the class preferred this milder version, oddly enough. They could see wanting to dump your wife because she was boring or ugly or a nag, or unsatisfactory in some other way;

they could understand the desire for a better model; but killing the first wife seemed extreme to them. They were nice boys, they intended to be doctors and so forth. Only pervs like the Duke would have to go all the way. "She would have been out of his hair, in a convent," said Bill. "She'd be happier in there anyway. The guy was a pain in the neck."

"I don't buy that," I said. "He definitely killed her. 'All smiles stopped together' – that's really sudden. It's pretty definite. But on the exam, you need to *say* there's the two choices. Anyway, he got rid of her. *Why*, is what the poem's about. What the Duke says is that she smiled too much."

"That's what I don't get," said Bill. "It's a really dumb reason. And there's another thing I don't get. If he's so smooth" – Miss Bessie had dwelt for some time on the Duke's smoothness, though she hadn't called it that, she'd called it cultivated and sophisticated – "if he's so smooth, why is he dumb enough to tell all this to the envoy? The envoy's just going to run back to the Count and say, 'Cancel the marriage – the guy's a dangerous creep!'"

I got up from the funeral-home wall, straightened down my skirt front and back, picked up my books. "We'll go through it again on Saturday," I told him. "I'll copy out my notes for you."

"I'm not going to pass it," said Bill.

At home, I lived in the cellar. I'd moved down there in order to study for my exams. The cellar was cooler than the rest of the house; also it was farther away from everyone else. These days I didn't feel like talking to anyone, or at least not to my parents. They didn't understand the gruesomeness of the ordeal before me, they thought I still had time to mow the lawn.

I slipped in through the back door and crept down the cellar stairs, unseen by my mother, and opened the freezer and took out the jar of Noxzema I kept in there. It was my theory that covering my face with frozen mentholated skin cream would stimulate the blood flow to my brain and make it more possible for me to study.

Once my face was entirely cold and white, I paced around my cellar room. I needed to get my thoughts in order, but the Duchess was eluding me. Maybe she hadn't been poisoned after all. Maybe she'd been stabbed with a poignard, or else strangled – not with a nylon stocking, as was habitual in the detective stories, but with a silken cord. Maybe she had been garrotted. This method also involved strangling; I didn't know what kind exactly, but I liked the sound of it. The poor girl, I thought. *Garrotted*, and all because she smiled too much.

But also – said the poem – hers wasn't any old kind of smiling. Her smile had "depth and passion" and was "earnest." I could see – now I was considering it at length – that a wife who went around smiling earnestly to left and right could have been annoying. There were girls at school who smiled at everyone in the same earnest, humourless way. In the school yearbook, it usually said about them, "Terrific personality" or "Our Miss Sunshine," but I'd never liked these girls very much. Their gaze slid over you, smile and all, usually coming to rest on some boy. Still, they were only doing what the women's magazines said they should do. *A smile costs nothing! A smile: the best makeup tip! Get smile appeal!* Such girls were too eager to please. They were too cheap. That was it – that was the Duke's objection: the Duchess was too cheap. That must have been his point of view. The more I thought about the Duchess and about how aggravating she must have been – aggravating, and too obliging, and just plain boring, the very same smile day after day – the more sympathy I felt for the Duke.

But there was no point in dwelling on the Duke's grievances: for the purposes of the final exam, he had to be the villain. Miss Bessie had told us to expect questions like, "Compare and contrast the characters of the Duke and the Duchess." For that, she said, we should prepare a list of opposites, arranged in acceptable pairs. I'd started on my own list:

Duke: ruthless, ~~stuck-up~~ proud, ~~oily~~ falsely polite, self-centred, shows off his money, ~~greedy~~ experienced, ~~psycho~~ art collector.

Duchess: innocent, modest, ~~smarmy~~ sincere, earnest, ~~sickly sweet~~ kind to others, humble, ~~stupid~~ inexperienced, art object.

A list like this would be a help to Bill. He'd be able to understand it, as long as I drew arrows from each of the characteristics on the *Duke* side to the corresponding characteristics on the *Duchess* one. My real, confusing thoughts I would keep to myself.

Bill's question about the envoy had stayed with me. It troubled me. Why indeed had the Duke spilled the beans in such a witless manner to a complete stranger if he was trying to convince the envoy to clinch the deal? *So, I want to marry the Count's daughter and this is what I did with the last Duchess I got my hands on. There she stands, as if alive.* Wink, elbow in the ribs of the envoy, get it? *Oh. Right*, says the envoy. *As if. Good one.*

The Duke wasn't an idiot. He must have had his reasons.

What if the arrangement had already been signed and sealed? If it had – if the wedding was a certainty – everything in the poem became clear. The Duke hated to explain things in person because explaining was beneath him, so he was using the envoy as a way of sending a message to the next Duchess, and the message was: *This is how I like my Duchesses to behave. And if they don't behave that way, curtains.* Curtains literally, because if this next Duchess got out of line, she too would end up as a picture with its own curtain in front of it. Who knew how many other pictures the Duke was keeping behind curtains, up there on the second floor?

The Duke was merely showing consideration by saying all this to the envoy: he wanted his likes and dislikes to be fully under-stood ahead of time – *only this much smiling, and only at me* – to avoid unpleasantness later. "'Just this/Or that in you disgusts me . . .'" he'd said. *Disgusts*: pretty strong language. He'd found the Last Duchess disgusting, and he didn't want to be disgusted by the next Duchess.

This was not the accepted view of the poem. The accepted view was that the envoy was horrified by what the Duke had told him and had tried to rush down the stairs first in order to get away from such a twisted nutbar. When the Duke said, "Nay, we'll go together down, sir," he was stopping the envoy from barging in front. But I didn't think so. I thought it more likely that the envoy had motioned the Duke to go ahead of him – probably he'd made a brown-nosing little bow – and the Duke had courteously set them on an equal footing. "We'll go together down, sir" – he was acting the pal. Most likely he'd put his arm around the envoy's shoulder.

If I was right, they were all three of them in cahoots – the Duke, the envoy, and the Count. The marriage was a trade-off: the Count would hand over the dowry and kiss the daughter goodbye, and would get social prestige in return, since Dukes rated higher than Counts. Once the Count's daughter had reached the Duke's palace – his *palazzo*, as Miss Bessie had told us it would have been called – she'd be all on her own. She couldn't expect help from her father, or from anyone else either. I thought of her sitting in front of her mirror, practising her smiling. Too warm? Too cold? Too much upward curve at the edges? Not enough? In view of the hints from the envoy, she'd be totally certain her life depended on getting that smile down perfectly.

On Saturday night I made my way over to Bill's, wearing my studying clothes: jeans and a sleeveless T-shirt, with a loose man's shirt over top. I went on my bicycle because Bill's parents were out in their car, or so he'd told me on the phone, so he couldn't pick me up.

Bill's family lived in a small, square, newish yellow-brick two-storey house; rows and rows of identical houses had been built in that area just after the war. The main bedroom was over the garage; there was a tiny vestibule, then a hallway that ran past the doors to the living room and the dining room to the boxy little kitchen. At the back there was a stuffy, cramped room with a La-Z-Boy recliner and a sofa bed that pulled out for guests, and the TV set; that room was where we did our studying when we were at Bill's. At my house, we did it at the dining table when my parents were home, and in the cellar when they weren't.

I rang the doorbell, Bill opened the door right away – he must have been waiting for me – and I stepped into the vestibule and slipped off my running shoes. This was a rule at Bill's house: shoes left at the door. Bill's mother had a job – she worked at a hospital, though she wasn't a nurse – but despite her job she kept the house spotless. It smelled of cleaning products – Javex bleach and lemon-oil furniture polish – with an undertone of mothballs. It was as if the whole house had been soaked in preservatives to keep it from ever changing, because change meant dirt. Bill and I never went into the living room, although I had looked into it. It had mole-coloured wall-to-wall carpeting and was crowded with varnished end tables, which in turn held an array of china figurines and crystal ashtrays, or were they bonbon dishes? The drapes were kept drawn to stop things from fading. There was no such roped-off, hushed, consecrated space in my own house.

Bill's mother didn't altogether approve of me. I'd learned about this kind of disapproval – the age-old disapproval of mothers toward any girl dabbling in their sons – from *Chatelaine* and *Good Housekeeping* (*Your Mother-in-Law: Best Friend or Worst Enemy?*), so I hadn't been surprised by the chilliness of her smile. On the other hand, whenever I encountered her she'd go out of her way to thank me for helping Bill study what she called "his English." It was a shame he had to study it – it wouldn't be any use to him later in life, and he got so discouraged about it; why couldn't he be allowed to focus on his strengths? – but since he did have to study it, better he should have a clever friend like me – she didn't say "girlfriend" – to keep his nose to the grindstone.

We started our studying well enough, going over the possible questions, and the answers to them, in point form. But then Bill said you needed to take a break from the books once in a while, and he went and got us some ginger ale, and soon we were fumbling around on the sofa bed. We didn't pull it out into a bed, however – only a cheap girl would have connived at such a thing, and also we were aware that Bill's parents might return unexpectedly, as they had done before. This evening they didn't return, but after a while we sat up anyway, and smoothed down our hair and did up our buttons, and went back to the studying.

Bill couldn't seem to focus. He grasped the list of opposite char-acteristics – that made sense to him. But then he said it was a shame, what that guy had done to the Duchess. She probably never even saw it coming, and then the smug little pervert had the nerve to brag about it, he'd stuck her picture up on the wall like a pin-up, most likely she was very good-looking as well, what a waste.

I said all of this was beside the point: the people marking the exam were not going to be interested in Bill's personal opinions. What they'd want was an objective analysis of the poem, using evidence. The poem would be printed right on the exam paper – they didn't expect him to have memorized it. All he had to do was read the question twice and make the accepted points – that stuff we'd been going over with Miss Bessie – and then find the lines in the poem that backed up those points, and then copy them down with quote marks around them.

Bill said yeah, he knew that, it's just that it was such a useless way of spending time and energy – what was it for in the end, what was it supposed to prove? I said it would prove he was an attentive reader, and that was all they wanted to know.

I shouldn't have said "attentive reader." It reminded Bill of his most recent run-in with Miss Bessie, and her sarcasm. His face went pink.

He said it was all pretty useless, because being an attentive reader wouldn't get him a job. I said it would, because that way he would pass the exam and he'd be able to go on. Anyway, I said, I didn't make the rules, so why was he mad at me?

Bill said he wasn't mad at me, he was mad at the goddamn Duke, for killing the Duchess. He ought to have been locked up or, better, hanged. So why was I defending him?

We'd had these kinds of stupid arguments before. They came out of nowhere, they went nowhere; during them each one of us would accuse the other of saying things that hadn't been said.

"I was not defending him," I said.

"Yeah. You were. She was a nice normal girl with a sick jerk for a husband, and you seem to think it was her own fault."

I hadn't said that, but it was partly true. Why did it make me angry to have Bill guess my feelings?

"She was a dumb bunny," I said. "She should have been able to figure out that he didn't like her smiling in that sucky way at every Tom, Dick, and Harry, and *sunset*, for heaven's sakes."

"She was just being friendly."

"She was just being a simp."

"She was not a simp. How was she supposed to know what he wanted? She couldn't read his mind!"

"That's what I mean," I said in a bored voice. "She was dumb."

"No, she wasn't! He was a creep! He never let on about the smile thing. He never said a word to her. It says in the poem. All that about choosing never to stoop."

"She was a half-wit."

"At least she wasn't a brainer and a show-off," said Bill offensively.

I said the Duke would have preferred a brainer and a show-off to a dumb bunny – a *disgusting* dumb bunny – because he was cultivated and sophisticated, he appreciated works of art. Anyway, I wasn't showing off, I was just trying to help him pass the exam.

"You think you're so smart," said Bill. "Thanks but no thanks. I don't need any goddamn help, and specially not from you."

"Okey-dokey," I said. "If that's what you want. Good luck." I gathered my books up off the floor and strode down the hall, as quickly as I could in my sock feet, and put on my running shoes in the vestibule. Bill didn't try to stop me. He stayed in the TV room. From the sounds coming out of it I knew he had turned on the TV.

. . .

I bicycled home in the dark. It was later than I'd thought. My parents were in bed with the lights out. I'd forgotten to take my key. I climbed up onto the garbage can beside the back door, twisted myself sideways, and slid into the house through the milk cupboard, a feat I'd performed many times before. Then I tiptoed downstairs and into my cellar room, where I burst into tears. Whatever temporary patching-up might take place, the era of Bill was now at an end. Bye-bye love, as in songs. All alone now. It was so sad. Why did such things have to disintegrate like that? Why did longing and desire, and friendliness and goodwill too, have to shatter into pieces? Why did they have to be so thoroughly over?

I could make myself cry even more by repeating the key words: *love, alone, sad, over.* I did it on purpose. After I'd finally finished crying, I put on my pyjamas and brushed my teeth, and covered my face with frozen Noxzema skin cream. Then I got into bed with *Tess of the d'Urbervilles*. Miss Bessie would be tackling it on Monday. It would be a full gallop for all of us, and I told myself I wanted to get a head start on it. In reality, I knew I wouldn't be able to sleep: I needed some distraction from my fight with Bill, which otherwise would have replayed itself over and over while I changed the words we'd spoken into other words that gave me more of an advantage, and tried to figure out what our actual words had meant, and then cried some more.

It didn't take me very much reading and skimming to discover that Tess had serious problems – much worse than mine. The most important thing in her life happened to her in the very first part of the book. She got taken advantage of, at night, in the woods, because she'd stupidly accepted a drive home with a jerk, and after that it was all downhill, one awful thing after another, turnips, dead babies, getting dumped by the man she loved, and then her tragic death at the end. (I peeked at the last three chapters.) Tess was evidently another of those unlucky pushovers, like the Last Duchess, and like Ophelia – we'd studied *Hamlet* earlier. These girls were all similar. They were too trusting, they found themselves in the hands of the wrong men, they weren't up to things, they let themselves drift. They smiled too much. They were too eager to please. Then they got bumped off, one way or another. Nobody gave them any help.

Why did we have to study these hapless, annoying, dumb-bunny girls? I wondered. Who chose the books and poems that would be on the curriculum? What use would they be in our future lives? What exactly were we supposed to be learning from them? Maybe Bill was right. Maybe the whole thing was a waste of time.

Upstairs, my parents were sleeping peacefully; they knew nothing of doomed love, of words spoken in anger, of fated separation. They were ignorant of the darker side of life – of girls betrayed in forests, of girls falling into streams and singing till they drowned, of girls done away with for being too pleasant. All over the city, everyone was asleep, drifting on the vast blue sea of unconsciousness. Everyone except me.

Me, and Miss Bessie. Miss Bessie, too, must have been up late. I couldn't imagine her doing anything as lax and unguarded as sleeping. Her eyes – not sarcastic eyes, I now realized, but merry eyes, the eyes of an elderly child, crinkled at the corners as if she were suppressing a joke or a quaint piece of wisdom – surely those eyes of hers never closed. Perhaps she was the one responsible for choosing our required reading material – she, and a group of others like her, all of a certain age, all with excellent suits, all with real stones in their lapel brooches, all with qualifications. They got together, they had secret meetings, they conferred, they cooked up our book list among them. They knew something we needed to know, but it was a complicated thing – not so much a thing as a pattern, like the clues in a detective story once you started connecting them together. These women – these teachers – had no direct method of conveying this thing to us, not in a way that would make us listen, because it was too tangled, it was too oblique. It was hidden within the stories.

I looked at my watch: three in the morning. I was so tired I was seeing double, but at the same time I was wide awake. I ought to have been brooding over Bill – didn't he require more tears? Instead, in the bright place at the back of my head, there was an image of Miss Bessie. She was standing in a patch of sunlight, which twinkled off her brooch, the amber-and-gold one in the shape of a bee. She had on her best suit, and a blouse with a crisp white bow, and her impeccable gleaming shoes. She seemed distant but very clear, like a photograph. Now she was smiling at me with gentle irony, and holding aside a curtain; behind the curtain was the entrance to a dark tunnel. I would have to go into the tunnel whether I wanted to or not – the tunnel was the road of going on, and then there was more of the road on the other side of it – but the entrance was where Miss Bessie had to stop. Inside the tunnel was what I was meant to learn.

Very soon I would be a last-year's student. I would be gone from Miss Bessie's world, and she would be gone from mine. Both of us would be in the past, both of us over and done with – me from her point of view, her from mine. Sitting in my present-day desk there would be another, younger student, who would be poked and prodded and herded relentlessly through the prescribed texts, as I had been. *The first line of a poem is very important, class*, Miss Bessie would say. *It sets the tone. Let us proceed.*

Meanwhile, I myself would be inside the dark tunnel. I'd be going on. I'd be finding things out. I'd be all on my own.

The Other Place

For a long time I wandered aimlessly. It felt like a long time. It didn't feel aimless, however, or not in any carefree way: I was being driven by necessity, by fate, like the characters in the more melodramatic novels I'd read in high school who would rush out into thunderstorms and lurk around on moors. Like them I had to keep moving. I couldn't help it.

I had an image of myself trudging along a dusty or lumpy or ice-covered road, carrying a little bundle on a stick, like the hobos in comic books. But that was much too droll. More like a mysterious traveller, striding inexorably forward, entering each new town like a portent, then vanishing without a trace, mission accomplished.

In reality I had no mission, and I did not trudge or stride. I went on the train, or – a treat at that time – on an airplane.

. . .

I would welcome each new dislocation, unpack my few belongings with alacrity and even joy, then set out to explore the neighbourhood or district or city and learn its ways; but soon enough I'd begin to imagine what I'd become if I stayed in that place forever. Here, a stringy-haired intellectual, pasty-faced, humourless, and morbid; there, a self-satisfied matron, shut up in a cage of a house that would not be recognized as a cage until it was too late.

Too late for what? To get out, to move on. Yet at the same time I longed for security. It was a similar story with men. Each one was a possibility that quickly became an impossibility. As soon as there were two toothbrushes – no, as soon as I could even picture two toothbrushes, side by side on the bathroom counter in trapped, stagnant, limp-bristled companionship – I would have to leave. My books would go into cardboard boxes and be shipped by bus, some getting lost on the way; my clothes and my towel – I did have a towel – would go into my small tin trunk. I hummed while I packed. Yet every time I began packing, it would feel like leaving home: my humming would alternate with fits of tearful nostalgia about the place I was doing the packing in, but that I hadn't even vacated yet.

As for my real home, the one I'd grown up in, I seldom thought about it, or not in any detail. I was dimly aware that I was a worry to my parents, but I resented their worry. I was doing fine. I was supporting myself. Every once in a while, an inner window would pop open and I would glimpse my parents, far away and very small, rushing through their daily activities as in a sped-up film: doing the dishes in a blur of soapy hands and cutlery, throwing themselves into bouts of maniacal gardening, making trips to their summer place with the car whizzing along as if jet-propelled; then doing the dishes there, then the gardening frenzy there, then back again, then into bed, then up with the dawn, round and round. They were immersed in mundane affairs, they were not contemplating any higher truths. I'd feel superior to them. Then I'd feel homesick. Then I'd feel like an orphan, a barefoot waif in the chilly night, peering in at scenes of cozy family life while filching a potato or two from the back plot. I would torture myself with these pathetic scenarios, then hastily shut the window again.

I was not an orphan, I told myself; I was not nearly enough of an orphan. I needed to be more of one, so I could eat food that was bad for me, stay up all night, wear unflattering clothes, and hang out with unsuitable companions, without the anxious running commentary this behaviour would call forth inside my head. *Why are you living in this dump? What are you doing with your time? Why are you with that creep? Why can't you accomplish anything? Get enough sleep! You'll ruin your health! Wear less black!*

None of these were things my parents would have said out loud – they knew better – but I believed in thought rays. These rays were shooting out from my parents' craniums, directly into mine. It was like radio waves. The farther away from home I got, the weaker the rays they were silently beaming at me would become. So I had to put a lot of distance between us.

Set against my desire for fecklessness was an opposite and more shameful desire. I'd never got over the Grade Two reader, the one featuring a father who went to a job every day and drove a car, a mother who wore an apron and did baking, two children – boy and girl – and a cat and a dog, all living in a white house with frilly window curtains. Though no house I'd ever lived in possessed such curtains, they seemed foreordained. They weren't a goal, they weren't something I'd have to strive for: these curtains would simply materialize in my life because they were destined. My future would not be complete – no, it would not be *normal* – unless it contained window curtains like these, and everything that went with them. This image was tucked away in a corner of my suitcase, like an emergency wardrobe item: nothing I wanted to wear at the moment, but worse come to worst, I could take it out, shake out the wrinkles, and step into it.

I couldn't keep up my transient existence forever. I would have to end up with someone, sometime, someplace. Wouldn't I?

But what if I missed a turn somewhere – missed my own future? That would be frighteningly easy to do. I'd make one hesitation or one departure too many and then I'd have run out of choices; I'd be standing all alone, like the cheese in the children's song about the farmer taking a wife. *Hi-ho, the derry-o, the cheese stands alone*, they used to sing about this cheese, and everyone would clap hands over its head and make fun of it.

Even I had made fun of the solitary cheese during that game. Now I was ashamed of myself. Why should being alone – in and of itself – be such a matter for derision? But it was. The alone – the *loners* – were not to be trusted. They were strange and twisted. Most likely they were psychopaths. They might have a few murdered corpses stowed away in their freezers. They didn't love anyone, and nobody loved them either.

In my more rebellious moments I asked myself why I should care about being shut out of the Noah's ark of coupledom – in effect a glorified zoo, with locks on the bars and fodder dished out at set intervals. I wouldn't allow myself to be tempted; I'd keep my distance; I'd stay lean and wolflike, and skirt the edges. I would be a creature of the night, in a trench coat with the collar turned up, pacing between streetlights, my heels making an impressively hollow and echoing sound, casting a long shadow before me, having serious thoughts about topics of importance.

Still, I was haunted by a poem I'd read at the age of twenty, written by a well-known poet much older than myself. This poem claimed that all intellectual women had pimples on their bums. It was an absurd generalization, I realized; nevertheless I worried about it. The frilly curtains I was destined to obtain and the pimply bum I was doomed to develop did not go together. Yet neither one had happened, so far.

Meanwhile I had to earn a living. In those times you could pick up jobs, do them for a while, put them down, then pick up something else, somewhere else. There was a shortage of labour, or a shortage of my kind of it, a kind that did not exactly have a name. I thought of myself as an itinerant brain – the equivalent of a strolling player of Elizabethan times, or else a troubadour, clutching my university degree like a cheap lute. I also – I felt – had the disreputability that came with such a position. At parties – faculty parties, during the times when the jobs I had were at universities, or company parties, when I peddled my skills in other sectors – I caught the faculty wives or the company wives eyeing me as if I had lice. Perhaps they thought I had designs on their husbands, though they needn't have worried about me.

The husbands were another matter. Any woman without a wedding ring on, no matter how dourly dressed, was free for a tryout in their books. Why did I never see them coming? But I didn't, I didn't edge away fast enough, and then there would be scuffles, in the kitchen perhaps where I'd be helpfully tidying up, or in the bedroom where the coats were piled, and then there would be outrage and hurt feelings, on everyone's part, it seemed. The husbands got angry because I'd drawn attention to their furtive trial gropings, the wives because I'd led the husbands on. As for me, I was less outraged than astonished. How could these pudgy or rancid elderly men possibly think they had any sort of allure? (This kind of astonishment is a function of youth. I got over it later.)

These attitudes and encounters were the norm in the early years of my ramblings. But then things changed. At the time I'd set out, all women were expected to get married, and many of my friends had already done so. But by the end of this period – it was only eight years, not so long after all – a wave had swept through, changing the landscape completely. Miniskirts and bell-bottoms had made a brief appearance, to be replaced immediately by sandals and tie-dyed T-shirts. Beards had sprouted, communes had sprung up, thin girls with long straight hair and no brassieres were everywhere. Sexual jealousy was like using the wrong fork, marriage was a joke, and those already married found their once-solid unions crumbling like defective stucco. You were supposed to hang loose, to collect experiences, to be a rolling stone.

Isn't that what I'd been doing, years before the widespread advent of facial hair and roach clips? But I felt myself too old, or possibly too solemn, for the love beads and pothead crowd. They lacked gravity. They wanted to live in the moment, but like frogs, not like wolves. They wanted to sit in the sun and blink. But I was raised in the age of strenuousness. Relaxation bored me. I thought I should be making my way in the world, wherever that was. I thought I should be getting somewhere – in my case, as things so often were, somewhere else.

During this period I lived in rooming houses, or in shared apartments, or in sublets. I had no furniture of my own: it would have slowed me down. I bought makeshift items at thrift stores in each new location and sold them when I left. I had no tableware. Now and then I'd indulge myself in a frill – a vulgar, colourful vase, a flea-market curio. I acquired a carved wooden hand holding a sort of chalice with the words *Souvenir of Pitcairn Island* on it. I splurged on a Thirties perfume bottle minus the stopper.

The objects I chose were designed to hold something, but I didn't fill them up. They remained empty. They were little symbolic shrines to thirst. I knew they were worthless clutter, but they made it into the tin trunk whenever I packed up again.

One year I got a job teaching grammar to freshmen at a university, which meant I could afford a real apartment, all to myself. The job was in Vancouver; the apartment was a top floor the family had built onto their bungalow for the purpose of renting it out. It had its own staircase, very steep and plain, with rubber runners and no banister or windows – more like a vertical tunnel than a staircase. It even had a few pieces of furniture – things the family below no longer had any use for. There was – for instance – a bed, covered with a bright green slippery satin bedspread of a kind that must have been thought glamorous twenty years or so before. There was a dressing table in a style that might have been Thirties. There was a gigantic gold-framed mirror. All of the furniture that came with the apartment was in the bedroom, which was like an old movie set or the cover of a paperback murder mystery of some years before. Satin bedspreads had been a feature of those. The corpse of the woman would be displayed surrounded by artfully rumpled satin, like a big flesh confection in a luxury box. In the gold-framed mirror would be the reflection of a man — just part of a man, his back turned, making his exit after the crime.

The apartment had a living room with a dining nook, and another room into which I put a Salvation Army desk and a chair and a typewriter. In the living room I set up a borrowed card table that acted as a dining table whenever I had any guests. For these affairs I used plates and cutlery, also borrowed.

I had a painting, bought from a friend of a friend because that person needed twenty-five dollars. The painting was an abstract, and showed some reddish blobs and scratches. When I'd had a few drinks I could see something in it, but without that sort of enhancement it looked like a damp patch on the wallpaper where something had leaked through. I hung it over the fireplace, which was not functional.

In this apartment, free at last from the eyes of roommates and far from the thought rays beamed out by my parents, I cycled through my most extreme versions of in and out, yes and no, stay and go, high and low, alone and together, elation and despair. One day I'd be flying through the clouds, drunk on cloudy possibilities; the next, up to my neck in mud, dragged down by the sodden prospects of the here and now. I walked around through the various rooms without any clothes on; I wore myself out reading until late in the night, then slept till noon, waking up entangled in the glossy green satin spread, unsure of where I was. I talked to myself; I sang out loud, silly, defiant songs I'd learned in school playgrounds a long time ago. *Hi-ho, the derry-o*, I'd sing. *The cheese stands alone! Tried the other place, tried the other place, tried the other place last night . . . There's a hole in the bottom of the sea, there's a hole in the bottom of the sea . . . I care for nobody, no not I, and nobody cares for me!* Or, deprived of all speech and song and even of motion, I'd find myself lying face down on the wall-to-wall carpeting of the hallway, through which I couldn't help hearing the derisive television laughter from the dwelling below. What if I died from starvation, right there on the carpet, through a simple inability to crawl to the refrigerator and get myself something to eat? Then all those fun-filled, roistering people on the television would be sorry.

In the evenings, when I wasn't twittering with glee or prostrate on the floor, I'd go for long, pensive walks. I'd start out purposefully, marching forward as if I had a destination. I was conscious of being watched through the windows of the floor below by the husband and wife who owned the apartment – he with a crewcut and a lawnmower, she with an apron and hair rollers. Although I dressed with relentless drabness, in dark browns and greys and shapeless blacks, they'd worried about renting to me until I'd proved I had a salary. It excited them to believe I was depraved in some way, or so I felt. I did have a lover or two during that time – temporary lovers, just borrowed – and they must have heard, on occasion, more than one pair of footsteps going up the stairs.

But for my evening walks I was alone. I made a point of it. As soon as I was out of the sight of the downstairs couple, I would slow down and choose the turnings at random, trying to avoid stepping on the huge black and grey slugs that crawled over the sidewalks as soon as it was dusk. These slugs ate everything, nothing ate them. There were advantages to looking unattractive.

But I wasn't without social resources. I didn't take off my clothes and sing in public: I acted in acceptable ways. I smiled, nodded, made conversation, and so forth. I could do a good imitation of a competent young woman. I had a number of friends and acquaintances, both male and female, of the kind that might be accumulated in a life of such transience. They would come for meals, sitting around my card table, drinking bottles of a local wine that dyed the dishcloth red whenever I'd get around to cleaning up. I learned how to make lasagna, a substance that cost little and went far. I also served a thing known as nuts and bolts, made with several kinds of dry cereal mixed with peanuts and Worcester sauce and toasted in the oven. That was a hors d'oeuvre, not a dessert. I had not yet taken up baking, so for dessert there was ice cream, bought at the corner store and so full of seaweed that when it melted it didn't turn to cream but to a gelatinous blobby substance that maintained its shape and was hard to wash down the drain.

One of the acquaintances who turned up to sit at my card table was a man called Owen. I didn't know him very well. He would ring the doorbell unannounced – I did have a doorbell – and I would go down the steep staircase and let him in. I might feed him some left-over lasagna, if I had any, or else some nuts and bolts. Then he would sit for long periods, not saying anything, as we both watched the long, lingering northwest summer sunsets turn from peach to pink to dark pink to the dull glowing red of a blown-out match.

Owen wasn't a lover or even a potential lover: nothing like that. He was in the city temporarily, like me, and had been loaded onto me by a do-gooder mutual connection (concerned, I now suppose, with his state of mind). He was alone, far more alone – I could see – than I myself had ever been. He had a desolation about him that I couldn't account for: sitting at my card table in the dusk was about the closest he could get to being with anyone.

Why did he keep dropping by? His presence was an enigma. He certainly wasn't bent on courtship. Neither did he want friendship. He wasn't demanding anything from me, but he didn't seem to be offering anything either. If I'd had a more lurid imagination — or if my lurid imagination was of the kind that attached itself to anything in the real world — I might have been afraid of him. I might have pegged him as a potential murderer. But I never made that sort of connection.

Despite the entire nullity of these evenings, it was hard to get Owen to leave. He would sit and sit, barely moving, inert, like a bundle of cloth, though topped with a head that was nevertheless alive, because the eyes moved. It was as if he'd been paralyzed in some appalling accident that had left no outward scars. His muteness was more exhausting than any conversation might have been.

I didn't want to say "I'm tired, I'm going to bed now." It seemed indelicate. Subtler hints were lost on him, but he wasn't a person I could be blunt with. I couldn't just say "Go home," as if to a dog. Somehow it would have been cruel. (Where was his home, anyway? Did he even have such a thing?) Eventually, when some inner timer had gone off in him, he'd get to his feet, thank me awkwardly for the lasagna, and trundle off down the stairs.

Finally one evening he told me that his three older brothers had tried to kill him when they were all children. Telling him it was a game, they'd shut him up inside a disused icebox and run away. Luckily their mother had noticed he was missing, and had tracked him down and let him out, just in time: he was already gasping and turning blue in the face. Probably his brothers hadn't meant to kill him, he said. They couldn't really have known what they were doing.

Owen related this episode in a flat voice, looking not at me but out the window at the dimming redness of the sunset. I was so thoroughly taken by surprise that I could not immediately think of anything to say. No wonder he was the way he was, I thought: what effect would a thing like that have on a person's life? To find yourself at an early age in a universe that had demonstrated such hostility would have a dampening effect. More than dampening: crushing. Could Owen be balancing on the edge of suicide? He'd said nothing about it, but people didn't always, or so I'd heard.

I felt I should respond in some emphatic way, declare a firm position, reach out a helping hand. My eventual murmur of "That's terrible" didn't seem nearly enough. Worse: I had a shameful desire to laugh, because the thing was so grotesque, as near-tragedies often are. Surely I lacked empathy, or even simple kindness.

Owen must have felt so too, because after that evening he never came back. Or possibly he'd done what he'd wanted to do: dropped off his anguish, left it with me like a package, in the mistaken belief that I would know what to do with it.

That image – of a little child being suffocated, or almost suffocated, by others who thought the whole thing was a game – melded with the furtive nocturnal slugs, and my solitary pacing and singing, and the separate, claustrophobic stairway, and the charmless abstract painting, and the gold-framed mirror, and the slithery green satin bedspread, and became inseparable from them. It wasn't a cheerful composite. As a memory, it is more like a fog bank than a sunlit meadow.

Yet I think of that period as having been a happy time in my life.

Happy is the wrong word. *Important.*

That was all quite long ago. I see it in retrospect, indulgently, from the point I've reached now. But how else could I see it? We can't really travel to the past, no matter how we try. If we do, it's as tourists.

THE OTHER PLACE

I moved out of that city, and then into another one, and then another. I had a lot of moves still ahead of me. Yet things did work out after all. I met Tig, and then followed the cats and dogs and children, and the baking, and even the frilly white window curtains, though they eventually vanished in their turn: they got dirty too quickly, I discovered, and were hard to take down and put back up.

I didn't become any of the things I'd feared. I didn't get the pimply bum I'd been threatening myself with, nor did I become a cast-out, wandering orphan. I've lived in the same house now for decades.

But my dreaming self refuses to be consoled. It continues to wander, aimless, homeless, alone. It cannot be convinced of its safety by any evidence drawn from my waking life. I know this because I continue to have the same dream, over and over.

I'm in the other place, a place that's very familiar to me, although I've never lived in it or even seen it except in this dream. Details vary – the space has many different rooms, mostly bare of furniture, some with only the sub-flooring – but it always contains the steep, narrow stairway of that distant apartment. Somewhere in it, I know – as I open door after door, walk through corridor after corridor – I'll come upon the gold mirror, and also the green satin bedspread, which has taken on a life of its own and is able to morph into cushions, or sofas, or armchairs, or even – once – a hammock.

It's always dusk, in this place; it's always a cool dank summer evening. This is where I'll have to live, I think in the dream. I'll have to be all by myself, forever. I've missed the life that was supposed to be mine. I've shut myself off from it. I don't love anyone. Somewhere, in one of the rooms I haven't yet entered, a small child is imprisoned. It isn't crying or wailing, it stays completely silent, but I can feel its presence there.

Then I wake up, and retrace the steps of my dream, and try to shake off the sad feeling it's left me with. Oh yes, the other place, I say to myself. That again. There was quite a lot of space in it, this time. It wasn't so bad.

I know the green bedspread isn't really a bedspread: I know it's some aspect of myself, some old insecurity or fear. I know the unseen child in the dream isn't my almost-murdered acquaintance, but only a psychic fragment, a tatter of my own archaic infant self. Such daylight knowledge is all very well. Still, why do I keep on having this dream? Maybe it served a purpose once, but I ought to be done with it by now.

Then I get up, and ask Tig how he slept, and we have toast and coffee together, and go about doing the many mundane and practical things there are to be done.

The dream frightens me, though. It brings with it a nebulous dread. What if it's not in the past, this other place? What if it's still in the future? After all?

Monopoly

Nell and Tig ran away to the country. Or as Nell told it later, Tig ran away to the country and after a while Nell joined him there. It was not a foregone conclusion. It could have turned out differently. Nell had been of two minds about going. She'd foreseen the difficulties. She'd had other choices. That was her story, one she came to believe as time went by and positions hardened.

In reality she hadn't foreseen any difficulties. She'd been sleepwalking. She'd been in love, a state of being she thought of as wiping the mind clean of any of the soothsaying abilities or even ordinary common sense it might otherwise have had. Moving to the country with Tig had been like jumping out of a plane, trusting that the parachute will open. And it must have been the right thing to do because Nell didn't end up lying smashed on the ground, and anyway here they are, here they both still are, after all these years. Once a certain amount of time has passed you can look back, you can laugh about things, she would say.

That was her other story, her second story; it played alternately with the first, like an old double bill at the movies.

Moreover, Tig didn't exactly run away. He ambled away. It was a slowed-down, freeze-framed movement, like a solitary Chinese person doing Tai Chi on a lawn. As any bank robber can tell you (Nell would say), the best thing to do when running away is not to run. Just walk. Just stroll. A combination of ease and purposefulness is desirable. Then no one will notice you're running. In addition to which, don't carry heavy suitcases, or canvas bags full of money, or packsacks with body parts in them. Leave everything behind you except what's in your pockets. Lightest is best.

Tig rented a farm, or what used to be a farm. The rent wasn't much: the man who owned it wasn't any sort of a farmer. He was a businessman – it was unclear what the business was – who hadn't decided whether he would turn the property into a weekend place for himself and his much-younger quasi-wife or else relocate in Mexico. He just wanted someone in the house so the local teenagers wouldn't break in and trash the place, as had been the case with several hapless absentee owners down the road. He didn't want to arrive some Saturday with a real-estate agent primed to evaluate the place and find FUCK YOU written in mustard from a squeeze bottle on the windows and human shit smeared on the walls and a scattering of roach ends and a smouldering hole in the wide-board pine floor. That was how he'd put it to Tig.

The businessman had already sold off most of the farmland. Only twenty acres were left – some fields, a woodlot. The fields hadn't been worked for some time, and Queen Anne's lace and sow thistles and burdocks, and saplings – hawthorns, native plums, wild apples – were growing up all over them.

There was a house with a lean-to shed at the back, and a huge barn with enormous beams and weathered planks and a tin roof. The house was on a hill, overlooking the pond that the businessman had put in. On the other side of the road was a line of giant hydroelectric pylons that stretched from one horizon to the other. You could think of it as spoiling the view or you could just incorporate it, Nell said to Tig, depending on how you felt about surrealism.

The house was a two-storey red-brick farmhouse with a centre gable – standard issue for the late nineteenth century in that part of the province, said *The Ancestral Roof* – a book Nell purchased and consulted frequently during her first winter with Tig, when she still thought life on a farm represented some superior form of authenticity. Originally, there would have been a parlour to the left of the front door, a kitchen and pantry to the right, and a back parlour opening off the kitchen, but the businessman had torn out some walls – to let in the light, he'd said. He'd installed a built-in kitchen table, and had painted the wallpaper white throughout, and had started stripping the chipped green enamel off the windowsills and mouldings, though he'd got only one window finished.

In a further outburst of interior decoration he'd cut a piece out of the main crossbeam of the barn, causing the barn walls to lean outwards – sooner or later the whole thing would collapse – and had stuck the section of barn beam as a mantelpiece over the cramped fireplace, which didn't work anyway.

A central staircase led up to the second floor. The stairs were uncarpeted wood, painted slate blue. There would have been four small bedrooms up there in the days of washbasins and tin tubs and outhouses, but one of these was now a drafty bathroom.

Of the three remaining bedrooms, one was Tig's, with nothing in it but a mattress on the floor. The second was reserved for Nell, as a sort of office or study — she needed a desk where she could spread out the page proofs she was working on. The desk was an old door laid across two filing cabinets, which gave her lots of room: they'd found the door in the shed and removed the knob, and the filing cabinets had come from a garage sale in the city, so the desk had cost almost nothing. This was good, because Nell did not make a lot of money, and most of Tig's income — sporadic at best — went elsewhere.

In addition to the desk, the office or study had a spare bed in it, a single bed that might also have been described as a couch or a daybed. It sagged in the middle and was covered with worn maroon velvet and smelled of wet dust, and Nell vowed that she would get rid of it or at least cover it up as soon as possible. When might *as soon as possible* be? When she had moved into the farmhouse, with Tig, finally; though every time she had this thought, she amended the *when* to an *if*.

The third bedroom had two double bunks in it: these were for the children and their visiting friends. The children were Tig's. It was on their account he'd run away so slowly and had not taken anything with him, and it was to them that most of his money was diverted.

What he'd run away from was his marriage. He'd had to get out of this marriage or it would have pulled him down, sucked the blood out of him, gutted him completely. All of these metaphors — suggestive, to Nell, of giant squid, of vampire bats, of fish processing — were Tig's. He had an oblique way of talking about his marriage, which in any case he did not do often. He never said *my wife* or used the wife's name in this connection, because it wasn't his wife as such that would have finished him off, it wasn't Oona all by herself that had done the pulling and sucking and gutting: it was the two of them together. It was *the marriage*, which Nell pictured as a large thorny growth – a cross between a dense, dark-green bush or shrub and a thundercloud-shaped cancer, with the adhesive qualities of tile cement and a number of tentacles, like a ball of leeches.

Nell felt intimidated by this marriage, and small and childish in comparison with it. It had a certain oversized and phosphorescent splendour about it, like a whale decaying on a beach. It made her seem pallid, at least to herself: pallid, banal, insipidly wholesome. She did not have nearly as much operatic and tenebrous and sanguinary melodrama to offer.

Tig's children came up to the farm on the weekends and slept in the bunk beds, with or without their friends. Both of them were boys – two blond-haired, angelic-looking boys, aged eleven and thirteen. Tig took pictures of them, and developed the pictures himself in the darkroom he'd set up in a curtained-off corner of the earth-floored farmhouse cellar, and showed the pictures to Nell: the kids in October, playing in the barn, jumping around on the piles of mildewed hay left over from the time of actual farming; the kids in early December beside the half-frozen pond, rocks poised in their mittened hands, about to throw the rocks at the ice; the kids in January, bundled up for winter, packing snowballs and smiling at the camera. Nell thought they looked happy enough.

Sometimes Oona drove up to the farm with Tig and the boys. She ate Saturday-night dinner with them, and went with the boys to inspect the barn, and watched them sliding on the ice, and slept on the musty single bed in Nell's workroom. This arrangement was supposed to make the children feel secure, said Tig: they needed to know they had two parents who both loved them very much, despite the thorniness and leechiness of the marriage. Nell was not there on those days, nor was she allowed to be there on any weekend, even when Oona didn't come up. Nell's presence (said Tig) would not be good for the children, nor even for Nell herself in the long run, as it might signal to the children that it was Nell who had destroyed the marriage.

She hadn't destroyed it, of course, said Tig: the thing was destruction incarnate long before she'd stumbled onto the scene. All of Tig's and Oona's friends knew this, they'd known it for years, and they'd admired the way Tig and Oona had worked things out so that life appeared to be going on in a normal way, said Tig. He also said he'd been so enraged one evening after an argument that he'd hurled every single one of their glassware and china items against the wall, leaving a pile of broken dishes to confront Oona in the morning. Nell was impressed by this gesture. She herself had never been good at impromptu rage. Throwing all the dishes at the wall was a fine and open act, much preferable to the white-faced silences and glum grudge-holding and resentful sulking she herself might have employed instead.

But Tig and Oona had been careful not to fight in front of the children, said Tig. They'd had a civilized arrangement on the outside, or civilized enough; they called each other "love" in public, and had sit-down Sunday dinners, with roasts – Nell herself had witnessed that. Thus the children would need some time to observe Tig living by himself in the country and Oona living by herself in the city before Nell could safely make an entrance, from the shadowy wings where she had been waiting.

So for the first part of that winter, Nell snuck around like a criminal on the run. She left no traces in the house when she wasn't there – no clothes in the small dark cupboard at the top of the stairs, no toothbrush on the inadequate shelf in the bathroom, no textbooks or lecture notes or page proofs on the improvised desk. Did Tig go through the house after she'd left, wiping her finger-prints off the doorknobs? It felt like that to her.

On Thursdays and Fridays, she had a temporary part-time teaching job at the university, filling in for a friend on sabbatical. She taught the Victorian novel to second-year undergraduates: the Brontë sisters, followed by Dickens, Eliot, and Thackeray, then the depressing realists, George Gissing and Thomas Hardy, with a decadent finale supplied by Oscar Wilde's *The Picture of Dorian Gray* and Henry James's *The Turn of the Screw*. She'd never taught this course before, so she had to read hard to keep ahead of the students. In theory, her Mondays, Tuesdays, and Wednesdays were reserved for the freelance editorial work that had been her intermittent mainstay over the past few years. The novel-reading and the editing were both things that she could do at the farm. On her non-teaching weekdays, she would take the Greyhound bus to Stiles, the town nearest the farm, then wait in the bus station on a hard wooden bench along a wall as if in a skating-rink change room, breathing in the gas fumes and cigarette smoke that permeated the chilly air. She would eat potato chips and drink black, acid-filled coffee and read about love and money and madness and furniture and governesses and adultery and drapery and scenery and death, until Tig would come along in his rusty blue Chevy to collect her.

Or she'd drive up from the city with him after he'd taken the children back in on Monday mornings – early, so they could get to school by nine. Nell and Tig could be at the farm in time for lunch, though during these drives Nell did not get hungry. Instead she felt light-headed and slightly ill, as she used to do before examinations. It was the anticipation, and the sense of being tested and judged, and the fear of failing. But what was it she might fail?

The car would be warm, and would smell of apple cores: the boys often ate apples in the car on the way to the city. Tig and Nell would hold hands, on the lonelier and less icy stretches of road. Instead of talking they would listen to the radio. At a certain distance from the city it was mostly country and western. Nell liked the songs of yearning, Tig liked the songs of regret.

The farm was on a gravel road, several miles from the main highway. In winter the farmhouse looked like a picture – snow on the roof, icicles dripping from the eaves, the white hills and sombre trees rising behind it – but it wasn't a picture Nell would ever have allowed on her Christmas cards. Like sunsets, it was beautiful in real life, but too overdone for art.

At the bottom of the long, curved, ice-covered driveway the car wheels would start spinning and the car would slew from side to side. Tig might take several runs at the hill, but he knew when to stop: it was important to avoid going into the decorative pond. If they couldn't make it up the drive, even with the aid of the bag of sand and the shovel Tig kept in the trunk, they'd leave the car at the bottom and crunch their way through the snowbanks at the sides of the drive, their breaths whitening the air, their noses dripping. It wasn't the best prelude to the romantic moment that was then supposed to follow once they'd gone in through the lean-to and the back door and stamped the snow off their feet and shed their boots and their heavy coats and their mittens and scarves.

Their other layers of clothing would be thrown off in Tig's gelid bedroom – insulation had not been a feature of the *Ancestral Roof* type of house, Nell had read – and then they'd be shivering under Tig's duvet, between Tig's threadbare sheets, locked in the sort of desperate embrace that reminded Nell of her Victorian novelists' descriptions of drowning. People drowned quite a lot in such novels, especially if they'd had sex out of wedlock.

After that would come an interlude of warm and languorous amnesia, followed shortly – for Nell – by disbelief: what was she doing here, in this situation? And what was the situation, exactly? She thought of herself as a person who liked things to be clear and direct and above-board, so how had she got mixed up in something so murky, and – if you looked at it objectively, from the point of view, say, of someone writing it up for the tabloids, should Tig and Nell be found asphyxiated in his car in a snowdrift because of carbon monoxide poisoning – so grubby? *Runaway Hubby Gassed Near Rural Love Nest with Editorial Cutie.* Although nothing like that had happened yet, and was unlikely to happen – neither of them was stupid enough to leave the motor running in a stranded car – the mere thought of it was humiliating.

Nell did not in any way let herself off the hook, being nothing if not self-critical, and anyway she was an adult – it was she who had chosen, it was she who had acted – but nonetheless the hard truth was that to some extent the whole thing was Oona's doing. Oona was the pivotal factor. Oona had set up the relationship, Oona had pushed it forward, Oona had made herself scarce at what turned out to be the critical moments, like some salacious Nurse figure out of a Shakespearean play. Why? Because Nell had suited Oona's purposes. Not that Nell herself had recognized those purposes at the time.

The first twosome had not been Nell and Tig, it had been Oona and Nell. They'd started out on fine terms. Oona could be very pleasant when she wanted to be: she could make you feel that you were her best friend, the only person in the world she could really depend on. Nell had been susceptible to that, as her image of herself had once included that kind of dependability. She'd been younger; younger than she is now, but also younger than Oona.

Nell had been Oona's editor in those days. She was already freelancing, ping-ponging her way among publishers caught short-handed. She'd carved a medium-sized niche for herself — she was known for working wonders with not-yet-publishable raw material, and for getting things in on time, and for not charging too much, and for fielding midnight calls from drunken authors with encouragement and tact and a form of murmuring that passed for understanding. Usually she edited novels. She'd taken on Oona's book as a trade-off for a publisher pal of hers, an old lover, in point of fact; he'd offered a plum in return for the root vegetable he considered Oona's book to be.

Yet Oona's book was the kind that publishers wanted, because it could potentially make money. In the time left over from her day job, which was as office manager for a smallish magazine, Oona had written a Superwoman self-help manual called *Femagician*, about how to juggle a career and a family and still find time for personal beauty routines and for remodelling the den. It was a subject that was fashionable just then, and the publisher was in a hurry: such waves had to be surfed before they'd passed by. They were counting on Nell — said her pal — to wrestle the book into shape in double-quick time.

Nell had spent many hours with Oona, recasting chapters and reorganizing paragraphs and suggesting fresh details and additions and deletions. She was surprised to find that, despite her outward appearance – briskness, tidiness, smiling capability – Oona's mind was like a sock drawer into which a number of disparate things had been shoved. There was a lot of jumble.

At the end of the editing process, the thing had been practically a different book, and certainly a better one, for which Oona had said she was grateful. She'd expressed this gratitude in the Acknowledgements section, and then again, in pen and ink, on the title page of the copy she'd given to Nell. *For invaluable Nell, the rewrite queen – the power behind the scenes. Love, Oona.* Nell had been pleased, because she admired Oona quite a lot, and looked up to her as an older woman who'd got her life figured out, unlike Nell herself.

The book had been a success, or what was considered a success then. Oona had been interviewed, not only in newspapers and on radio, but on television as well, on the kinds of morning chat shows for women that existed at that time. She'd become moderately and, as it turned out, temporarily famous. In the context of Oona's life – the editing sessions with Nell, and then the book's publication and its aftermath – Nell had seen Tig as an indistinct form, a shadow in the background. Nell had known nothing about Tig then, and nothing about the submerged horrors of the marriage: she was far outside the circle of friends who were in on the civilized arrangement.

In public, Oona'd had nothing but praise for Tig. He'd been so supportive of her career, she'd said. He helped with the grocery shopping, he did a lot of the cooking, he stayed with the kids when Oona was otherwise occupied, and all of that in addition to his job at the radio station where he worked as a producer of documentaries and interviews. Unlike the jealous monsters that turned up in newspaper headlines for beating their wives to death with crow-bars or drowning them in the bathtub, he was entirely in favour of her having a life of her own.

The two of them had appeared, glossily coloured, in the pictures taken for a magazine article. They were pretending to cook a meal together – possibly not even pretending. Oona was stately in a loose caftan garment, a necklace of uncut amber around her neck, Tig large and ruggedly casual in a vest and shirt sleeves. The magazine was a women's magazine, so shots of the kitchen were featured. A raw turkey was posed between them, with carrots and potatoes and celery stalks surrounding it in an artful arrangement. They made an imposing couple, Nell had thought wistfully: at that time they'd represented the kind of stability lacking in her own life. She'd been discovering recently that she was a more conventional person than she'd once imagined herself to be.

Then Oona had wanted to write another book, a follow-up to the first one. Actually, she'd wanted Nell to write it: she, Oona, would dictate her thoughts into a tape recorder, and Nell could do the useful, necessary work of transmuting these thoughts into print. The book was to be called *Femagician's Box of Tricks*, which was – Nell agreed – a good title, even if it did sound a bit like a children's fantasy adventure. The trouble was that Oona seemed unsure about what she wanted to include in the box. Some days the book sounded like a memoir, other days like a do-it-yourself – how to get white rings off the furniture, what to do about ink spots on the rug – and on yet other days it resembled a manifesto. Of course, it could be all three, Nell said – there were ways of doing that – but Oona had to make some preliminary decisions about goals and intentions. Here Oona had wavered. Couldn't Nell do that? Because Oona herself was so busy.

During the time of these — what were they? Skirmishes? Pleadings? Negotiations? — Oona had done some confiding in Nell. (Nell thought she was being specially favoured, let in on something very private — Oona had a way of dropping her voice that suggested secrecy — but she found out soon enough that this was not the case. Oona's secrets were open secrets, her recital of them a frequently repeated ritual.) Her marriage to Tig, said Oona, wasn't a real marriage any longer. The two of them slept in separate rooms, they'd been doing that for years. They were staying together for the sake of the children: Tig had been wonderful about that. They had a gentleman's agreement about what Chaucer's Wife of Bath had called "other company." Oona had tossed off the reference lightly: a lesser practitioner would have made more out of it, used it perhaps to show off, but Oona was more sophisticated than that.

Sophisticated was the word that came to mind when Nell thought of Oona. Oona had true furniture, a blend of Victorian, with a heirloom aura about it, and pared-down modernist; she also had genuine pictures on the wall, with frames. She had some signed and numbered prints. Nell did not aspire to this level: her one-bedroom apartment had a table and two chairs, one of them a cheap beanbag, and a baggy corduroy-covered sofa, and four bookcases with her accumulation of books, and a single bed with squeaky springs — all thanks to the Salvation Army and the Goodwill shop — and a couple of posters stuck to the walls with tacks. She was saving up her money, though she wasn't sure what she was saving it for. She'd gone so far as to paint the table orange and add two throw pillows to the sofa, but she saw no point in exerting herself any further because the apartment was only a stopover, like the many other apartments and rooms she'd camped in before it. She wasn't ready to settle down, she told her friends.

That was one way of putting it. Another way would have been that she had not found anyone to settle down with. There had been several men in her life, but they hadn't been convincing. They'd been somewhat like her table — quickly acquired, brightened up a little, but temporary. The time for that kind of thing was running out, however. She was tired of renting.

After the conversation about the separate rooms and the gentleman's agreement, Nell went back to her one-bedroom and sat at her Sally Ann table with her college Chaucer and looked up the Wife of Bath reference, just out of curiosity. The Wife of Bath was not exactly an adulteress, as Oona technically was: the "other company" consisted of men she'd played around with before marriage, not during it. But that was quibbling. Anyway, no one used the word *adultery* any more; it was not a cool word, and to pronounce it was a social gaffe. It had been banished somewhere around 1968; now, three years later, long-term marriages were still blowing apart for no visible reason, middle-aged men with respectable jobs were still smoking dope on weekends and wearing wooden love beads and ending up in bed with girls half their age, and once-contented homemakers were still jumping ship and starting new careers, and, in extreme cases, turning into lesbians overnight. Once, there had been no lesbians, or none to be seen, but suddenly they were bursting out all over. Some of them weren't even real lesbians; they were just getting back at their husbands for the love beads and the young girls.

The young girls themselves, as well as the wives in escape mode, signalled their open-mindedness by their clothing. They wore overalls and glasses with big round frames, or else folkloric ankle-length skirts and thick-soled sandals; they had long straight picture-book hair or curly ethnic mops or very short crops; they ringed their eyes in black and had pale pink lipstick, or else they used no makeup at all. "Love is love," they would say, with a smiling but doctrinaire manner that Nell found self-righteous. *Love is love.* It sounded very simple. But in practical terms, what did it mean?

Nell liked to know the rules, whatever the game: she was a stickler for rules. As a child she'd separated her food into piles: meat here, mashed potatoes there, peas fenced into a special area reserved for peas, according to a strict plan of her own. One pile could not be eaten before the one already started had been consumed: that was the rule. She didn't even cheat herself at Solitaire, which she'd spent quite a lot of time playing over the years.

As for social interactions, she had learned only the old rules, the ones in force up to the explosive moment – it seemed like a moment – when all games had changed at once and earlier structures had fallen apart and everyone had begun pretending that the very notion of rules was obsolete. By the former rules, you did not steal other women's husbands, just for instance. But there was no such thing as husband-stealing now, it appeared; instead there were just different folks doing their own thing and making alternate life choices.

Nell had spent the period of upheaval feeling bewildered and disoriented and out of her depth. To have confessed to such a thing, however, would have been to attract contempt. She'd felt alone in her reaction, and had kept her mouth shut, and had left literary parties early so as not to have to struggle with bearded men in hallways and fend off stoned individuals of either sex in gardens lit with Japanese paper lanterns and listen to their slurred but angry pronouncements on her uptight mode of being.

Her affairs – *affairs*, another obsolete word – her *relationships* before this moment had at least had plots. They'd had beginnings and middles and ends, marked by scenes of various kinds – in bars, in restaurants, in coffee shops, and even – when things had got extreme – on sidewalks. Despite the necessary pain, and the tears shed – usually by herself – there had been something satisfying, though not enjoyable, about such scenes: after them Nell had frequently felt congratulations were in order, as if parts had been played as written and unspecified duties discharged.

There had been entrances and exits then, not just the vague wanderings in and out of rooms and the mumblings and slouchings and shrugs that had replaced social life. Emotions with recognizable words attached to them had been involved: *jealousy*, *despair*, *love*, *treachery*, *hate*, *fault*, the whole antique shop. But to have a vocabulary of any size was now a disadvantage, among the young and those who purported to be young.

Oona and Tig were older than Nell. They had not discarded the old rules completely, they still went in for talking. Shortly after the Wife of Bath episode, Oona invited Nell to dinner – one of the convivial roast beef dinners Oona and Tig were apparently famous for. Nell went off to the dinner in good faith, hoping that there would be chairs around a proper dining table, instead of the agglomerations of brown rice and the random grazing that were the fashion at more addled or bohemian gatherings. She'd seen the table, she'd done some editing sessions with Oona at it. Even at the worst, there would be place settings; at the very best, no people sitting cross-legged on the floor and monologuing about their acid trips. There was another couple there – a history professor and his wife, miraculously still together. The professor had been in one of Tig's documentaries, and was an authority on the Seven Years War.

The two children had had their dinners earlier but appeared for the special dessert, a Grand Marnier soufflé with chocolate sauce.

The atmosphere was festive, if a little supercharged. Oona and Tig turned bright, interested faces toward Nell whenever she spoke, which wasn't often – mostly it was the history professor who held forth. Still, when Nell did find something to say, she didn't feel she had to sift through her words and pick only the short ones.

After dinner, the history couple left and Nell helped Oona carry the dishes out to the kitchen – that was one of the old rules – and then she played a game of Monopoly with the two boys. They were friendly and polite, and treated her as if she were a somewhat older child. She shook the dice and rolled them, and was lucky, and acquired not only the water works and the electric company and all four railways and some blocks of red streets and pale-blue and purple slum property, but Park Place and Boardwalk as well, on which she built hotels. Although surprised by her own ruthlessness – it was only a game, she should let the children win – she then charged high rents, and ended by driving the kids into bankruptcy and winning the game.

Impressively, the children did not sulk, but wanted to play again, though Oona declared that it was too late for that. Then they had ice cream, and two of the three family cats climbed up on Nell and purred. Nell felt charmed, and welcomed, and accepted, and somehow protected, with Tig and Oona beaming down at her and the boys like the kindly fairy godparents in some tale of rescued orphans.

The dinner invitation had been proffered so that Nell could get the full benefit of Tig. This was a conclusion Nell came to later. She was being interviewed, in a way: Oona had her fingered for the position of second wife, or if not a second wife exactly, something second. Something secondary. Something controllable. A sort of concubine. She was to serve as Tig's *other company*, so that Oona could get on with the life of her own she was so determined to lead.

What had happened next? Nell wasn't quite sure. She'd been swept off her feet, evidently. She'd been swept away. Or possibly she'd been kidnapped. Sometimes it felt like that. Whatever it was had played a part in Tig's flight to the country, though no one had said so.

In late January, Nell bought some knitting wool, red and blue and purple. She hadn't done any knitting for a long time, not since childhood, but she had an urge to take it up again. Her idea was to knit a wool bedcover for the seedy bed in her so-called study, the bed Oona slept in when she came up to the farm to visit on weekends. She would knit it in long strips, a red square, a purple one, a blue one, and then she would sew the strips together. It would take some planning to make it come out right, with the squares creating the bold checkerboard effect she had in mind. Once she had the bedcover done she would put it on the bed, and there it would stay.

Maybe she would do that. On the other hand, maybe she wouldn't. Maybe she would go back to her orange table and her Sally Ann sofa, taking her knitting with her. She hadn't decided.

When Tig wasn't there — when he'd gone off on some excursion or other — she would read, or edit manuscripts, or she would mark student papers. The Notion of the Gentleman in *Great Expectations*. Governesses in *Jane Eyre*, *Vanity Fair*, and *The Turn of the Screw*: Drudge, Fortune Hunter, Hysteric. Conformity and Rebellion in *The Mill on the Floss*. But her study was on the north side of the house: it got chilly, and darkened early. So she would take long breaks from whatever she was doing, and make herself cups of tea, and sit beside the sunny window that had once been the front parlour's, knitting away at her blue and red and purple bed covering and listening to the dripping of water from the eavestrough icicles, and gazing out toward the line of dazzling white snowdrifts curving across the field, and the row of cedars behind them, and the blue shadows. At these times she could forget that she had any decisions yet to be made. She felt lazy and soothed, as if she were floating in a warm bath. But then she would have to pinch herself, and return to a state of alertness, and make an attempt to consider her position.

What exactly was it that Tig was offering her? He claimed to want permanence, but in what form? He was still married, after all. There would be a plot, there would be emotions and events, that much was predictable. There would be love – the word had been used – but what kind of love was it? And in terms of daily life, what did it mean? "I think it could work out for us," was how Tig had put it. "I want to share my life with you." But did the life he said he wanted to share include – for instance – Oona?

Nell could feel Oona's presence as soon as she walked through the door of her study. Feel, or possibly smell: Oona favoured perfumed cosmetics, leaning toward the more exotic end of the aroma spectrum. During their editing days Nell had found these scents pleasant enough, but now she couldn't settle down to work unless she opened the window first to let in a current of fresh air, despite the sub-zero temperatures. She had the sensation that Oona was standing just behind her, looking over her shoulder, smiling in an ambiguous manner and giving off waves of soporific odour, like a field of ripe poppies.

But Oona had been coming up to the farm less and less, according to Tig. As for the project of Oona's new book, the one Nell was to have edited, or – more like it – ghost-written, it had been quietly dropped.

. . .

In late February, Tig announced that it was now time for Nell to be at the farm at the same time as the boys. Nell wasn't sure she was ready for that. She'd got used to being invisible: to change the arrangement now would be to upset a balance. But Tig said he'd explained about her to the boys, about how she was living at the farm for most of the week, so she had to do her part. Anyway he and Oona had discussed it and had agreed that this was the way things should go: it was time for the boys to see Nell on her home turf.

"Why did you discuss it with her?" asked Nell, making her voice as neutral as possible.

Tig looked baffled. "Naturally I discussed it with her," he said. "We discuss everything about the boys. She's their mother."

"What exactly did she say?" said Nell. "About me?"

"She's all in favour of it," said Tig. "She's all in favour of *you*. She thinks you'll be good for the boys."

"But what about me?" asked Nell. She wanted to add that the farm wasn't her home turf. She didn't have a home turf, she wasn't settled, she hadn't made up her mind. She wanted more courtship.

"What do you mean?" said Tig.

"Who do they think I am?" said Nell. "What am I supposed to be?"

"You're supposed to be the wonderful woman who lives here with me," said Tig. He wrapped his arms around her and kissed her neck, but she could tell that he was annoyed nonetheless. She was making difficulties where none existed. She was overstepping a line. But where was the line? She couldn't see it.

. . .

MONOPOLY

On the last Saturday in February, Nell took the Greyhound bus up to Stiles. It was already the afternoon: Tig and Oona had decided that Nell shouldn't try to spend the entire weekend, not the first time, because it might be too much of a strain for the children. She waited in the station for Tig to pick her up, knitting away at her bedspread. She had only two more rows of squares to go; she'd already attached the finished rows together, using a crochet hook, and the red and purple and blue checkerboard effect had come out just the way she'd pictured it.

Tig was late, but this was nothing new. He was usually late collecting her. He had other errands to do in Stiles. He needed to get gas, go to the hardware store, buy groceries. Once she'd recognized that, she was fine about the lateness, more or less.

They drove to the farm in the rusted-out Chevy. The boys were sliding around on the frozen pond. They didn't have skates on, but they had hockey sticks; they were shooting pucks. They waved their mittened hands as the car skewed its way up the drive.

This time there was no embrace, no throwing off of garments, no hurried plunge under Tig's duvet. Instead, once they were inside the door there was an awkward pause.

"They'll be happy out there for a while," said Tig.

"Maybe we should make some cocoa," said Nell. That was what you did with children: you made them cocoa. "And popcorn," she added. Those were the foods that had been served up for her when she was a child, on cold winter afternoons such as this one: comforting foods, rich and sweet and warm.

"That's a good idea," said Tig. He smiled at her, pleased that she was making an effort.

Luckily there was some cocoa, and also some popping corn. Nell busied herself mixing up the cocoa powder and the sugar. She measured the milk into a saucepan, then she turned on the stove and began jiggling the corn kernels in an iron pot. Den mother, she thought. Camp counsellor. Sunday-school teacher on an outing. Those were her choices, her disguises: prissy ones, all of them, reeking of blue cotton blouses with badges on their sleeves. How would she greet the boys? "Hello there, I'm your dad's mistress." But *mistress* as a word had gone out the window along with *adultery*. You couldn't have the one without the other.

The boys came in through the shed; she could hear them laughing, stamping the snow off their feet. Then they were in the main room. They looked at her shyly, with what might also have been distrust or apprehension: much the same way – Nell supposed – that she was looking at them. Then they shook her hand, each one in turn. Despite the thorniness and leechiness of the marriage that had been their habitat until now, they had been what used to be known as well brought up. They were taller than she remembered them, and older, but of course they would be. It was months – a lot of months – since she had last seen them.

The three of them sat at the kitchen table, drinking their cocoa and eating their popcorn and playing Monopoly, while Tig boiled up spaghetti for dinner. The game did not have the spontaneity of their first game together; the moves were more cautious, more guarded; the boys hoarded their Monopoly money as if for some future emergency. There wasn't the same reckless acquisition of property, the same gambling and risk-taking. Possibly they were remembering their first game with Nell, back when both parents were still under the same roof pretending that all was well. Now it was the boys who had to pretend that all was well. Tig was pretending too: he was overly jolly, vibrating with anxiety. He so much wanted everything to go smoothly.

MONOPOLY

Nell played as sloppily as she could and made numerous loans, but she won the game anyway despite her best efforts. She couldn't bring herself to cheat. (In the months to come, she and the boys, and sometimes even Tig, would play many more such games. Nell tried to substitute Hearts or group Solitaire, but the boys demanded Monopoly. Nell felt sorry for them: each boy wanted to win, just once. But they had bad luck, and it could not somehow be managed.)

While they were eating their spaghetti, Oona phoned. After a few exchanges with Tig and a conversation with each of the boys, she asked to speak with Nell. Nell came to the phone reluctantly. It was a wall phone, right in the kitchen. Tig and the boys went still: they couldn't help listening.

Oona's voice had the confiding though authoritative tone Nell remembered. "You will make sure they do their homework, won't you?" she said. "Tig lets them play around too much. They're getting behind at school."

So that's who I'm supposed to be, thought Nell. I'm the governess.

At the end of March, when the snow was mostly gone except in the shadows, and the buds were swelling, Nell finished her bedspread and arranged it on the single bed in her study. She was pleased with the way it had turned out. She called Tig in to admire it.

"Does this mean you're here to stay?" asked Tig, folding his long arms around her from behind. Nell didn't say anything, but she smiled. He wasn't so obtuse after all.

In April, the boys brought up one of their cats because a farm needed a cat: they'd seen some mice, or possibly rats, in the barn. The cat was a city cat. Not being used to travel, it growled and threw up in the car, and when they'd reached the farm it leapt out before anyone could grab it and ran off into the bushes and wasn't seen for days. When it came back it was thinner and had burrs stuck all over its fur. It scooted under the bed in Nell's study and wouldn't come out. Evidently, however, it must have emerged at night and rolled around on Nell's knitted bedspread, to which it transferred most of the burrs. Nell picked away at them, but she could never get out all the little hooks and prickles.

Moral Disorder

There's never been such a lovely spring, Nell thought. Frogs — or were they toads? — trilled from the pond, and there were pussy willows and catkins — what was the difference? — and then the hawthorn bushes and the wild plums and the neglected apple trees came into bloom, and an uneven row of daffodils planted by some long-vanished farmer's wife thrust up through the weeds and dead grasses beside the drive. Birds sang. Mud dried.

In the evenings, Nell and Tig sat outside their rented farmhouse on two aluminium-framed lawn chairs they'd found in the back shed, holding hands, slapping away the occasional mosquito, and watching a barred owl teach her two young to hunt. For practise they were using the twelve ducklings Tig had bought and installed on the pond. He'd made a shelter for the ducklings — like a little house without walls, set on a floating raft. They could have gone in under the roof and been safe, but they didn't seem to know enough to do that.

The owl swooped down in silence down over the surface of the pond where the ducklings ignorantly paddled, snatching a duckling a night, carrying each one up to the cavity in the dead tree where she had her nest, then rending the duckling apart and sharing it out to the young to be gobbled down, until all twelve ducklings were gone.

"Look at that," said Tig. "Such grace."

At the beginning of May the businessman who owned the farm said he was selling it. He gave them a month to move out. Since there wasn't any lease, they had to go. But they couldn't move back to the city, they were agreed on that. It was just too beautiful up here.

They drove a half hour farther north, where the prices would be cheaper, and scouted around on back roads, searching out the For Sale signs. Up near Garrett they managed to find something in their price range: a house, a barn, and a hundred acres. It had been on the market for more than a year. Vacant possession, said the owner, who was showing them around himself. He lived on another farm; he'd been using this barn to store hay. But now he was selling both properties, cashing in. "I want to see a bit of the world before it's time for me to be putting on the wooden overcoat," he said.

There was a pond on this farm as well, and a number of gnarled apple trees set around the house, and a drive shed with an old tractor in it. That came with, said the owner. The house was white clapboard, built in the mid-1830s, with a cement-floored addition on the back — a summer kitchen. The cellar was unfinished; its beams were trees with some of the bark still on them. The steps down to it were steep and hazardous. The dirt floor was damp, and had a hard-to-place odour. Not dry rot, not dead mouse, not sewage, exactly.

"It needs a lot of work," said Nell. The farmer cheerfully admitted it, and knocked five thousand dollars off the price. Then there was the matter of the mortgage, said Tig: they were iffy propositions for a bank, since neither of them had a permanent full-time job. But the owner said he would give them a mortgage himself.

"He's in a hurry to get rid of this place," said Nell. They were standing in the middle of the kitchen floor, which sloped steeply down toward the centre wall: they'd have to jack the floor up from underneath and run in a new crossbeam, sooner or later. The wallpaper — one of many layers, as could be seen by the torn parts — was a faded green, with bulbous pinkish-brown flowers on it. The floor was linoleum-covered, in a pattern of maroon and orange oblongs Nell recognized from the Fifties.

"There's a hundred acres," said Tig.

"The house is kind of dark," said Nell. "It's not very cheerful."

"We'll clean the windows," said Tig. No one had lived in here for years. Dust and dead flies coated the windowsills. "We'll paint the wallpaper white." He'd been out with the farmer, walking over the land. He'd seen a marsh hawk in the back field; he treated it like an omen.

Nell didn't say it wasn't the windows, not the wallpaper. But paint would help.

They scraped together the down payment, using Nell's savings and a sum from a television documentary Tig had recently put together. The weekend after they'd closed the deal, they moved their bed in. Then they sat on the linoleum floor, eating sardines out of the tin, and slices of brown bread and hunks of cheese, and drinking red wine. There was only a single glaring overhead light bulb dangling from a wire, so they turned it off and lit a candle instead. It was like an indoor picnic.

"So, it's all ours," said Tig.

"I've never owned any real estate before," said Nell.

"Neither have I," said Tig.

"It's a bit scary," said Nell.

"We'll go out and see the hawk tomorrow."

Nell kissed Tig. It wasn't the best idea because of the sardines, but they'd both been eating them.

"Let's go to bed," said Tig.

"I need to brush my teeth," said Nell.

They lay on Tig's mattress – their mattress – with their arms around each other. They'd carried the candle upstairs; it flickered in the warm breeze that came in through the open bedroom window. Nell thought about filmy white curtains – she'd always wanted those, when she was young – and about how such curtains would ripple in such a breeze, once they had some.

"You shouldn't have said I'm your wife," said Nell after a while. "At the lawyer's."

"A lot of women are keeping their own names now," said Tig.

"But it's not true. Oona's your wife. You're still married to her."

"Not really," said Tig.

"Anyway, you put *spouse* instead of *wife*. It's a dead giveaway. Didn't you catch the way he was looking at me? That lawyer?"

"What way?"

"Just that way."

"What would you like to be called?" said Tig. Now he sounded hurt.

Nell said nothing. She was spoiling things; she didn't want to. She'd been put in a false position, and she hated that. But she had no other word to suggest — no word for herself that would be both truthful and acceptable.

Over the next few days, they moved in the rest of their possessions — the bunk beds for Tig's two children, the ones they slept on when they came to visit; the single bed for the guest room; Nell's desk; a few chairs; some bookcases and books. Nell's orange table. She'd left the rest of her furniture behind in the city. They'd have to get some other furniture eventually — the house looked quite empty — but they didn't have the spare cash for it at the moment.

Tig's two boys came up the next weekend and slept in their bunk beds in their new room and went for a long walk with Tig, all around the property. They saw the marsh hawk — two marsh hawks. They must be a pair, said Tig; they'd been hunting for mice. The boys were pleased with the tractor in the barn. You didn't need a licence to drive a tractor, not if you didn't go out onto the road. Tig said that when he'd got the tractor in running order — or when someone had — the boys could drive it around the fields.

Nell didn't go on the walk. She stayed in the house and made biscuits. There was an old electric range that worked perfectly well except for one burner. They were going to get a wood stove too. That was the plan.

When Tig and the boys got back, they all ate the biscuits, with honey on them, and drank tea with hot milk in it. They sat casually around Nell's orange table with their elbows on it, just like a family.

I'm the only person here who isn't related to anyone, thought Nell. She was feeling cut off. She didn't get into the city very often any more, and when she did it was on business – she met with publishers, and with the authors whose books she was editing – so she didn't see her friends very much. In addition to which, her parents weren't speaking to her, as such, though they weren't not speaking to her either. Conversationally, she'd been put into a grey zone, a lot like a bus station waiting room: cold air, silences, topics limited to states of health and the weather. Her parents hadn't got used to the fact that Nell had actually moved in with a man who was still married to someone else. She'd never been so blatant, in her former life. She'd given some thought to appearances. She'd been sneakier. But now that her change of address cards had so flagrantly been sent, there was no comfort room left for sneakiness.

Nell threw her energies into a kitchen garden. There were groundhogs in the fields, so she began with a fence; Tig helped with it. They set the bottom edge of the chicken wire a foot into the earth so the groundhogs couldn't tunnel under. Then Nell dug in a lot of the well-rotted cow manure from the heap she'd found in the barn. There was enough of it to last for years. Beside the front door there was a knobbly, straggly rose; she pruned it back. She pruned some of the apple trees too. She'd taken a new interest in sharp implements – shears and clippers, picks and shovels, pruning saws and pitchforks. Not axes; she didn't think she could handle an axe.

By this time she'd read up on the local pioneers – the people who'd arrived in the area in the early nineteenth century and had cleared the land, chopping down the trees, burning their trunks and branches, arranging their gigantic roots into the stump fences that were still to be seen here and there, slowly decaying. Many of these people had never used an axe before they'd come. Some of them had chopped off their legs; others had stood in buckets while using their axes in order to avoid that fate.

The soil of the garden was good enough, though there were a lot of stones. Also shards from broken crockery, and medicine bottles of pressed glass, white and blue and brown. A doll's arm. A tarnished silver spoon. Animal bones. A marble. Layer upon layer of lives lived out. For someone, once, this farm had been new. There must have been struggles, misgivings, failures, and despair. And deaths, naturally. Deaths of various kinds.

While Nell worked in the garden, Tig went out and about. He drove up and down the side roads, exploring. He went into Garrett and tried out the hardware store, and set up an account at the bank. The in-town grocery store – not to be confused with the boxy new supermarket on the outskirts – had a sign in the window for eggs: BONELESS HEN FRUIT. On his return from these excursions, he'd tell Nell about such discoveries, and bring her gifts: a trowel, a ball of twine, a roll of plastic mulch.

There was a combination gas station and general store at the nearest crossroads; Tig began to drink coffee there with the local farmers, the older ones. They viewed him as an oddity, he said. They hadn't tossed him into the bin of contempt to which they consigned most people from the city. He drove a rusty car and didn't wear a tie and knew what a ratchet set was: all to the good. But he wasn't a farmer either. Nonetheless, they let him sit in on the coffee sessions, where he picked up farming hints and gossip. They even began teasing him a bit, a development he reported to Nell with some glee.

Nell didn't go along on these jaunts; she wasn't invited. The rule for the farmers' coffee group was men only. This was not stated, it was a given.

"I asked them what sort of animals we should have," Tig said one day after coming back from the store at the crossroads.

"And?" said Nell.

"They said, 'None.'"

"That sounds like a good idea," said Nell.

"Then one guy said, 'If you're going to have livestock, you're going to have dead stock.'"

"That's probably true," said Nell.

After several days, Tig said that if they were going to live on a farm, they ought not to let the land go to waste, and that would mean having some animals. Also it would be added value for the boys to learn where food really came from. They could start with chickens: chickens were easy, said the farmers.

Tig and the boys built a somewhat lopsided chicken house so the chickens could be protected from predators at night. They also made a fenced-in yard where the chickens could run around safely. Tig and Nell and anyone else who was there would be able to eat the eggs, said Tig, and then they could eat the chickens themselves, once they got too old to lay eggs.

Nell wondered who was going to kill the elderly chickens when the time came. She did not think it would be her.

The chickens arrived in burlap sacks. They adjusted to their new surroundings immediately, or they appeared to: they didn't have a wide range of facial expressions. The farmer who'd supplied them had thrown in a rooster. "He said the hens would be more contented that way," said Tig.

The rooster crowed every morning – an ancient, biblical sound. The rest of the time he stalked the hens while they were scratching in the dirt and pounced on them from behind and stomped up and down on them. If Nell or the boys got too close to the hens when they went into the yard to collect the eggs, the rooster would jump on their bare legs and rake them with his spurs. They took to carrying sticks, to hit the rooster with.

Nell made the chickens' eggs into pound cake, which she froze in the freezer they'd found themselves buying, because where were they going to keep all the stuff that would be produced by the kitchen garden once it really got going?

Then Tig got some ducks – not ducklings, this time – which were allowed to fend for themselves in the pond, and then two geese, which were supposed to lay eggs and produce goslings; but one of the geese injured its leg, so it had to be taken up the road to Mrs. Roblin.

Tig and the boys and the Roblins were now friends, though Nell suspected the Roblins – the senior Roblins, who ran a dairy operation, and the junior Roblins too, of which there were many – laughed at them behind their backs. The Roblins had been on their farm for a long time, and knew what to do about all farm emergencies. The nearby cemetery had a lot of Roblins in it.

Mrs. Roblin was a square-shaped, round-faced old woman – Nell thought she was old – with short but surprisingly strong arms and red, deft, stubby fingers that (Nell suspected) had never seen the inside of a rubber glove. The boys said she pitched in when necessary, and Nell understood that this pitching had nothing to do with baseball and everything to do with manure. Mrs. Roblin was clearly capable of any kind of enterprise involving guck and muck and blood and innards – the boys had seen her reach up into a cow and pull a calf out, legs first, a sight that had filled them with awe. While telling this, the boys would look at Nell, not critically, but dismissively: there was no way Nell would ever find herself up to the elbows in a cow's vagina, said that look.

Nell had hoped Mrs. Roblin would set the goose's leg and put a splint on it, but that wasn't what happened. The goose came back in oven-ready form, which, said Tig, was the way things were done in the country. The remaining goose, or was it a gander, wandered around for a while, looking sad, thought Nell, and then flew away.

By this time there were also two peacocks, a pair Tig had found at a peacock farm on one of the back roads and had given to Nell as a present.

"Peacocks!" Nell said. Tig was intending to please her. He always did intend it. How could she not appreciate his enthusiasm, his spontaneity? "What about the winter?" she said. "Won't they die?"

"Peacocks are a northern Himalayan pheasant," Tig said. "They'll take care of themselves. They'll be fine in the cold."

The peacocks were always together. The peacock would display, unfurling his huge tail and rattling it, and the peahen would admire him. They flew around easily, and sat in trees, and pecked about here and there. Sometimes they flew into the hen yard. The rooster knew better than to get into a fight with the peacock, which was a lot bigger than him. At night, the peacock couple roosted on the crossbeam of the barn, where they must have thought they were out of danger. They screamed like babies being murdered, usually just before dawn. Nell wondered where they would make their nest. How many baby peacocks would they produce?

In the garden, Nell planted everything she could think of. Tomatoes, peas, spinach, carrots, turnips, beets, winter and summer squash, cucumbers, zucchinis, onions, potatoes. She wanted generosity, abundance, an overflowing of fecundity, as in Renaissance paintings of fruitful goddesses – Demeter, Pomona – in flowing robes with one breast bare and glowing edibles tumbling out of their baskets. She put in a herb garden with chives and parsley and rosemary and oregano and thyme, and three rhubarb plants, and some currant bushes, a red and a white, and some elderberry bushes so they could make elderflower wine in the spring, and a bed of strawberries. She planted runner beans that were supposed to grow up tripods made of poles.

The local farmers did not recognize this bean method. On their regular sightseeing forays into the yard – there was always an excuse, a stray dog, the loan of a wrench or hammer, but really they just wanted to see what Tig and Nell were up to – they looked hard at the structures of bare poles. They didn't ask what these were. When the beans started creeping into view, they stopped looking.

"Hear your cows went on a spree again," they would say. They had a way of staring at Nell sideways: they couldn't figure her out. Were she and Tig married, or what? The way they half-grinned at her said they didn't think so. Maybe she was a free-lover, some sort of hippie. That would fit in with her busting her ass in the garden. Real farm wives didn't have gardens. They loaded their pickups with groceries once a week from the supermarket in Garrett, twenty miles to the east.

"Hear it took three days to get them cows back in the barn. Maybe you should take 'em to Anderson's."

Nell knew what Anderson's was. It was the abattoir: Anderson's Custom Slaughtering. "Oh, I don't think so," said Nell. "Not yet."

They had the cows because Tig had decided they should raise their own beef: the coffee-drinking farmers all did. "Raise four, sell three, put one in the freezer, you're all set," was their pronouncement. So Tig purchased four Charolais-Hereford crosses on credit from one of these helpful farmers, who didn't tell any actual lies, but it would have been better for Nell and Tig if they'd asked a few informed questions. They didn't know that the cows would be able to jump, and jump so high.

The fences had to be raised and strengthened, but sometimes the cows got out anyway and ran off to join a large herd of other cows nearby. Tig had to take the two boys to get them back – throw some ropes on them, wrestle them into the truck they'd borrow for the purpose. That was dangerous, because the cows were skittish and never wanted to come home.

"Maybe they know we're going to eat them," said Nell.

"Cows want to be with other cows," said Tig. "They're like shoppers."

The cows' names were Susan, Velma, Megan, and Ruby. The boys had named them. They were warned about doing that – humanizing the cows – but they did it anyway.

Oona always telephoned on the weekends. At first she'd wanted to speak to Nell as well as to Tig and the boys – she wanted to enlist Nell's help, and issue instructions – but after a while she'd stopped doing that. Once in a while curt messages were relayed to Nell from Oona, via folded and sealed notes delivered by the boys. Usually they concerned missing socks.

One of the hens escaped from the yard and was found among the rhubarb plants with her throat slit. "Weasel," said Mrs. Roblin, having inspected the wound. "They drink the blood." She asked if Nell wanted to take the hen home and stew it, as it was still fresh and the blood had been let out. Nell did not – the victim of a weasel murder was surely tainted – so Mrs. Roblin kept the hen, saying she could think of a use for it.

Another hen set up shop behind a jumble of machinery parts in the drive shed, where she hoarded eggs – her own, and those of other hens avoiding their brooding duties. By the time Nell found her, she was sitting on twenty-five eggs. What could be done? The eggs were too old – too well developed, too full of embryos – to be eaten.

The boys were going to spend the rest of the summer at the farm, said Tig – a last-minute arrangement, because Oona was going on vacation. She was heading for a Caribbean resort, not alone.

"Do you mind?" Tig said, and Nell said of course not, though it would have been nice to have been told ahead of time. Tig said there hadn't been any ahead of time.

Nell stuck a list onto the refrigerator with a magnet. It was a list of cleaning duties: sweeping, clearing the table, washing the dishes. They would all take turns. She herself would continue to do all the laundry, in the temperamental second-hand wringer machine they'd found; she'd continue to hang it on the line. She was already baking the bread, and the pies, and making the ice cream, with some of the extra eggs and the cream they were getting up at Roblins'. Also there were the currants to be considered – she couldn't make every single currant into jelly. She'd tried to dry some of them in the sun, but then she'd forgotten about them and it had rained. Despite the various lists she'd been making, she couldn't keep track of everything.

There were numerous auctions that season — farmers died or sold up, and then everything in the house and barn would be put on the block. Nell felt like a scavenger; still, she went. She got a couple of quilts that way — they needed only a little mending — and a wooden chest, with missing hinges, but those would be easily fixed once she got around to it. She wanted things that would add up to a look — a farm look. More or less olden days.

Tig bought a baler, dirt cheap because it was an out-of-date kind. It produced small oblong bales — not the outsized cinnamon buns of hay that were the fashion now. He and the boys would take off the hay, he said. They could feed it to the cows in the winter and sell the excess hay at a dollar a bale. He'd pay the boys, of course — whatever you'd pay an unskilled labourer. Tig and Nell would lose money on this venture, or break even at best, said Tig, but it would be a terrific experience for the boys, who would be able to do some real work and feel useful. What did Nell think of that?

"I think it's fine," said Nell. This had become her standard answer when it was a question of Tig's enthusiasms.

While Nell and Tig were going to farm sales, the boys spent time in the barn. They got up to lots of things in there. Alcohol was consumed, psychedelic substances tested, cigarettes and dope smoked regularly. The dope came from local back fields, where some of the younger farmers were growing lucrative though illegal crops of what they called "wacky tobaccy." Inside the barn, plots were hatched. Making off with the car was considered, running away to Montreal, or at least to Garrett, to see horror movies. These plots remained theoretical, and the boys did not shout or smash things, unlike some Nell had heard of, so Tig and Nell had no idea. They found all this out much later, once the boys had grown up, and had passed through their twenties and their anger at Tig for having left home, and had begun to share their reminiscences.

The boys weren't getting on too well at school – Oona had forwarded their report cards, implying that this lack of progress was Tig's fault. But Tig – who had the tractor working now, who let the boys drive it around the farmyard and out to the back field – said they were learning so many other things, things that would come in handy for them in their later lives.

The boys were taller now – taller than Nell. One of them was almost as tall as Tig. They had tans, and biceps; they ate huge meals, and when Tig didn't have them working at something else they were under the tractor, unscrewing parts of it and screwing them on again. They got covered with grease and oil and dirt and sometimes blood from various tool-inflicted wounds, which seemed to make them quite happy. Nell washed a lot of towels.

When the weather was right – hot and sunny – and the hay had been cut and raked into rows, Tig and the boys laboured at the baling, wearing thick gloves and bandanas twisted around their foreheads to keep the sweat from running into their eyes. The baler got dragged around the fields by the tractor, spewing out bales and chunks of dried mud and pieces of twine. The process was hot and dusty, and very noisy. Straw made its way into their clothes, fragments of it went up their noses. Getting the bales into the barn was the worst part. Nell helped sometimes, wearing a bandana and a big-brimmed hat. In the evenings they were all so tired they could barely eat; they fell into bed before sunset.

At the end of August, Tig received a typed letter from Oona, accusing him and Nell of exploiting the boys as child labour in order to make a profit from them.

. . .

Tig and Oona were supposed to be drawing up a separation agreement so they could get a divorce, but Oona kept changing lawyers. She thought that because Tig and Nell owned a farm, Tig must be lying to her about his income. She wanted more money. But Tig didn't have any more.

Nell sensed that she was growing a hard shell, all around herself. It kept her from feeling as sorry for Tig as she ought to. Tig's view was that he couldn't get into any sort of open conflict with Oona. He could not, for instance, initiate a divorce. Oona must be allowed to believe that she was the one in control. If Tig did anything sudden – if he made the first move – Oona would use it against him with the children. After all, they lived with her, officially; not with him.

"They spend more time with us," Nell said. "If you count waking hours. And she'll use it against you anyway. She already is."

"She isn't well," Tig said. "There's something wrong with her health." He said that nothing must be done to disturb Oona unduly.

I disturb her unduly anyway, thought Nell. I can't help it.

There was more to this conversation, but it wasn't voiced.

I'm almost thirty-four, thought Nell. When will things be untangled?

But Tig was in no hurry.

The wild plums in the hedgerows ripened and fell. They were blue, ovoid, fragrant. Nell gathered them up by the basketful and carried them home in a swirl of tiny fruit flies, and made them into compotes and rich purple jam. Tig licked her purple fingers, kissed her purple lips; they made love slowly in the warm, hazy evenings. Replete, thought Nell. That's the word. Why would I want anything to change, ever?

In September, Nell picked the less wormy and scabby apples from the apple trees and made them into apple jelly. The ground under the trees was littered with fallen and fermenting apples: butterflies lit on them and drank, then staggered around unevenly; wasps did the same. One morning Tig and Nell woke up to find a herd of drunken pigs lying under the trees, grunting and snoring in contentment. Evidently they'd been on a binge.

Tig chased them off, then followed them to see where they'd come from. They were from the pig farm up the hill, in back: they did this every year, said the pig farmer. They'd break out of their pen, just as if they'd been planning it for months, and dig their way under the fence. They always picked the right time. It cheered them up to have this one orgy to look forward to, was his view. Never mind that the apple trees weren't his.

Nell knew they couldn't say anything. A boundary was a boundary only if you could defend it. People's houses got broken into around here. Theft took place, vandalism. She didn't always feel safe when Tig wasn't there.

Susan the cow went away in a truck one day and came back frozen and dismembered. It was like a magic trick – a woman sawed in half on the stage in plain view of all, to reappear fully restored to wholeness, walking down the aisle; except that Susan's transformation had gone the other way. Nell didn't want to think about what had happened to Susan during her period of invisibility.

"Is this Susan we're eating?" said the boys, shovelling down the pot roast.

"You shouldn't have named the cows," said Nell. The boys grinned. They'd discovered the value of shock and horror, at least at the dinner table.

Nell was overrun with vegetables. She didn't know what to do with them. Some could be canned, others dried and frozen, yet others – such as the mound of surplus zucchinis – fed to the chickens. Nell put up a dozen jars of cucumber pickles, a dozen jars of pickled beets. She stored the potatoes and carrots and onions in the root cellar, where they joined the bottles of homemade beer Tig had brewed and the crock of fermenting sauerkraut from Nell's excess cabbages. Putting the sauerkraut in the cellar was a mistake – it filled the whole house with a strong odour of dirty feet – but Nell comforted herself with the thought that it was high in vitamin C and would be useful if they were snowed in all winter and began to get scurvy.

In the second week of October, Tig and Nell beheaded their first hen. Tig did it with the axe, looking a little pale. The hen ran around in the yard, spouting blood from its neck like a fountain. The cows became agitated, and mooed. The remaining hens cackled. The peacocks screamed.

Nell had to consult Mrs. Roblin as to what to do next. She scalded the hen and plucked it, as per instructions. Then she took out the insides. She had never smelled anything so nauseating. There were a number of eggs, of various sizes, in various stages of development.

That's it, she thought. I'm not doing this again. Those chickens will die of old age as far as I'm concerned.

Tig made the chicken into a stew, with carrots and onions from the garden. The boys ate it with relish. They wished they'd been there to see the hen running around without a head. Tig had recovered from his pale moment and was revelling in the joys of description.

In late October, three ewes were added to the cows in the farmyard. Tig's idea was that they would produce lambs, which could then be sold or eaten. The ewes waded into the pond for some unknown reason and got their legs tangled in a roll of barbed wire that was lurking under the surface, and Tig had to cut them free with wire cutters and carry them out. Their fleece was sopping wet and they were very heavy. They struggled and kicked, and Tig slipped and went sideways into the pond, and after that he got a cold. Nell rubbed Vicks VapoRub on him, and made him hot lemon with whisky in it.

In November, Tig's bottles of homemade beer began to explode, down in the cellar. There would be a bang, then beer and broken glass all over the floor, like a Saturday-night car crash. Nell never knew when one of the bottles was about to go off: venturing into the cellar to get a carrot or a potato was like running a minefield. But the beer in the bottles still intact was excellent, said Tig, though very effervescent. He had to drink those bottles in quick succession so they wouldn't be wasted.

Winter came. The driveway drifted over; the car had to be left at the bottom of the hill, where the big snowplow coming by regularly buried it. Then there was a sleet storm, and the telephone wires came down, and the electricity went off. Luckily the wood stove had been set up by then. Nell and Tig huddled beside it, wrapped in quilts, burning a flock of candles to keep the darkness at bay.

On other days — days without blizzards, or high winds, or freezing rain — the fields were dazzlingly white and pure, the air crisp. Tig loved feeding the animals on such days; he found it peaceful. They'd gather around him in the morning while he opened a fresh bale of hay, their fragrant breath steaming in the cold, jostling one another only slightly, looking in the wintry scene like the corner of a Nativity tableau. Nell gazed out the window at the tranquil grouping, feeling she was back in a simpler time. But then the phone would ring. She'd hesitate before answering: it might be Oona.

In February, with the snow whipping across the icy fields, the ewes lambed. One of them had triplets, and rejected the smallest of her three lambs: Tig found it shivering and trembling in a corner of the stall. Tig and Nell took the disowned lamb inside the house and wrapped it in a towel and put it into the wicker laundry basket, and wondered what to do next. Unfortunately, one of the lambs left with the ewe stuck its head between two boards in the stall and froze to death, so in theory the third, runty lamb could have replaced it; but the mother would have nothing to do with the desolate little creature.

"It must smell wrong to her," said Nell. "It's been with us."

Mrs. Roblin told them to put the wrapped-up lamb inside the oven with the door open and the heat on low and feed it brandy with an eye dropper, so that is what they did. She came over in person to make sure they were doing it right. She treated Nell and Tig as if they were slightly dim-witted children — a few bricks short of a load, as the local farmers were in the habit of saying. The lamb was bleating feebly and kicking a little; Mrs. Roblin looked into its eyes and then its mouth and said it would most likely make it through. Nell wanted to know how she could tell, but felt it would be stupid to ask.

Day by day the lamb grew stronger. Nell cradled it in her arms while feeding it; she was embarrassed to find herself rocking it and singing to it.

"What's its name?" said the boys.

"It doesn't have a name," said Nell. She wasn't going to fall into the trap of naming it.

Soon the lamb was standing up, drinking milk from a baby bottle. Tig made it a stall in the summer kitchen, where it was given fresh straw bedding every day; but as it became friskier and wanted to run and leap, they decided it was a shame to keep it cooped up, so they let it into the house. On the slippery linoleum – the new, slippery linoleum they'd laid down, with a pattern in the shape of tiles – its four legs splayed out and it had trouble keeping its balance. But soon it had mastered the art, and was bouncing here and there, twirling its long woolly tail.

It couldn't be toilet-trained, however. It peed whenever it felt the urge, and left piles of shiny brown raisin-sized pellets on the linoleum. Nell made it a diaper out of a green plastic garbage bag, cutting holes for the back legs and the tail, but that was worse than useless.

At the end of March, the peahen was found dead on the floor of the barn, underneath its crossbeam perch. A weasel must have gone up there during the night, said Mrs. Roblin: weasels would do that. The peacock was hanging around the crumpled body, looking confused. What will become of him now? thought Nell. He's all alone.

. . .

By April, the lamb was too big to be kept in the house. He was becoming too strong, too boisterous. They put him into the barnyard with the cows and sheep, but he didn't make friends with the other lambs. He kept to himself, except when Tig went into the yard to feed the animals. Then, when Tig's back was turned, the lamb would take a run at him and slam into him from behind.

It was a different story with Nell. When she appeared, the lamb would come over to her and nuzzle against her; then he'd stand between her and Tig.

Tig had to take a length of two-by-four into the barnyard to defend himself. When the lamb came running at him he'd whang it on the forehead. The lamb would shake its head and back off, but soon enough he would try again.

"He thinks it's a contest," said Nell.

"He's in love with you," said Tig.

"I'm glad somebody is," said Nell.

"What's that supposed to mean?" said Tig, aggrieved.

Nell didn't know what it was supposed to mean. She hadn't intended to say it. It had just come out of her mouth. She felt her lip trembling. This is ridiculous, she thought.

After the murder of his wife, the peacock started behaving strangely. He displayed to the hens in their yard, fanning out his tail, rattling the feathers. When the hens showed no interest in him, he leapt on them and pecked them. He had a powerful neck, and packed a hard wallop. He killed several hens.

Tig shut the hens up in their house and tried to catch the peacock, but he flew away out of reach and screamed. Then he went after the ducks, but they had the sense to skitter down into the pond where he couldn't get at them. Then he caught sight of his own reflection in one of the house windows — a window with a mound of earth near it, on which he could stand. He displayed to himself, fanning and rattling his tail feathers and screaming in threat, and then attacked the window.

"He's gone mad," said Tig.

"He's in a state of grief," said Nell.

"It must be mating season," said Tig.

The peacock took to lurking around outside the house, peering in through the ground-floor windows like a crazed voyeur. He knew his enemy was in there. Hate had replaced love in his tiny, demented head. He was bent on assassination.

"We should find him another mate," said Nell. But they didn't get around to it, and then one day he was gone.

The lamb was growing bigger and bigger and more and more fearless. He no longer waited until Tig's back was turned, he'd now charge at him from any angle. His skull seemed made of cement; hitting him with a two-by-four merely encouraged him.

"We can't let him go on like this," said Tig. "He's going to injure someone."

"He thinks he's a human being," said Nell. "He thinks he's a man. He's just guarding his territory."

"All the more reason," said Tig. There was a farmer nearby — said the guys at the store — who'd been drinking one night and had tried to cross a field where a billygoat was pastured. The goat ran at him and knocked him down. Every time the poor sod tried to get up, the goat knocked him down again. By sunrise the poor bastard was almost dead. The lamb would soon be a full-grown ram; then he might pull something like that.

"So what are we going to do?" said Nell. They both knew what. But Tig wasn't up to chopping the head off the lamb, and then dismembering it, or whatever had to be done; he wasn't up to butchery. Hens were as far as he would go.

"We'll have to take him to Anderson's," he said.

They managed to catch the lamb. Nell had to lure him over to where Tig waited stock-still with a rope, because the lamb trusted her and didn't see her as a rival. Once they'd wrestled him down to the ground, they tied his legs together and carted him out of the barnyard. The other sheep and the cows looked over the fence, mooing and baaing. They all knew something was up.

Tig and Nell lifted the lamb into the trunk of the Chevy. He kicked and struggled, and bleated piteously. Then they got into the car themselves and drove away. Nell felt as if they were kidnapping the lamb – tearing him away from home and family, holding him for ransom, except that there wouldn't be any ransom. He was doomed, for no crime except the crime of being himself. His muffled bleats did not stop, all the way to Anderson's Custom Slaughtering.

"What next?" said Nell. She felt exhausted. Treachery is hard work, she thought.

"We get him out of the car," said Tig. "We take him into the building."

"Do we have to wait?" said Nell. While it's happening, she meant. While it's being done. The way you'd wait at a child's first visit to the dentist.

Wait where? There was no place to wait.

Anderson's was a long, low building that had once been white. The double doors were open; from inside came a dim light. Stacks of barrels stood around outside in the yard, and crates, and a closed van — a horse van — and some rusted machinery parts. A sort of pulley. The barrels and crates also looked rusted, but they couldn't be rusted because they were made of wood.

There was nobody around. Maybe they should honk the horn to announce their presence, Nell thought. That way they wouldn't have to go in.

Tig was at the back of the car, trying to get the trunk open.

"It's jammed or something," he said. "Or maybe it's locked." From inside the trunk the lamb bleated.

"I'll go in," said Nell. "There must be someone. The doors are open. They'll have a crowbar." Or something, she thought. They'll have all kinds of things. Bludgeons. Sharp-edged tools. Knives for the throat-slitting.

She went into the building. A row of naked light bulbs hung from the ceiling. Beside the door were two more barrels, the tops off. She looked in: they were filled with skinned cows' heads, in brine. She assumed it was brine. There was a sweet, heavy, clotted smell, a menstrual smell. The cement floor was strewn with saw-dust. At least the weather is cool, she thought. At least there aren't a lot of flies.

Farther on was a sort of corral, and some high-sided pens or cubicles.

"Hello?" she called. "Anybody here?" As if she'd come to borrow a cup of sugar.

From around the corner of one of the pens came a tall, heavy man. On top he was wearing nothing but an undershirt; his thick arms were bare. As in some old comic book about torturers in the Middle Ages, he was bald. He had an apron on, or maybe it was just a piece of grey canvas tied around his middle. There were brown smears on it that must have been blood. In one hand he was holding an implement of some kind. Nell did not look closely at it.

"Help you?" he said.

"Our lamb is stuck in the trunk," she said. "Of our car. It's jammed shut. We thought maybe you had a crowbar or something." Her voice sounded tinny and frivolous.

"Won't be hard," the man said. He strode forward.

On the way back to the farm, Nell began to cry. She couldn't stop. She cried and cried, without restraint, in gasps and sobs.

Tig pulled over to the side of the road and stopped the car, and took her in his arms. "I feel sad too," he said. "The poor little fellow. But what else could we do?"

"It isn't just the lamb," said Nell, hiccupping, wiping her nose.

"What is it then? What?"

"It's everything," said Nell. "You didn't see what was in there. Everything's gone wrong!"

"No, it hasn't," said Tig, hugging her tightly. "It's all right. I love you. It'll be fine."

"It won't, it won't," said Nell. She began to cry again.

"Tell me what it is."

"I can't!"

"Just tell me."

"You don't want me to have any babies," said Nell.

. . .

The lamb came back in a white oblong cardboard box, like a dress box. Neatly arranged in waxed paper were the tender pink chops, the two legs, the shanks and neck for stewing. There were two little kidneys, and a delicate heart.

Tig cooked the lamb chops with dried rosemary from Nell's garden. Despite her sorrow — for she still felt sorrow — Nell had to admit they were delicious.

I am a cannibal, she thought with odd detachment.

Maybe she would grow cunning, up here on the farm. Maybe she would absorb some of the darkness, which might not be darkness at all but only knowledge. She would turn into a woman others came to for advice. She would be called in emergencies. She would roll up her sleeves and dispense with sentimentality, and do whatever blood-soaked, bad-smelling thing had to be done. She would become adept with axes.

White Horse

In their second year at the farm, Nell and Tig acquired a white horse. They didn't buy this horse, or even seek her out. But suddenly, there she was.

In those days they picked up animals the way they picked up burrs. Creatures adhered to them. In addition to the sheep, cows, chickens, and ducks, they'd gathered in a dog they called Howl – a blue tick hound, possibly even a thoroughbred: he'd been wearing an expensive collar, though no name tag. He'd wandered in off the side road – dumped there by whoever had mistreated him so badly that he rolled over on his back and peed if anyone spoke a harsh word to him. There was no point in trying to train him, said Tig: he was too easily frightened.

Howl slept in the kitchen, sometimes, where he barked in the middle of the night for no reason. At other times he went on excursions and wasn't seen for days. He would come back with injuries: porcupine quills in his nose, sore paws, flesh wounds from encounters with – possibly – raccoons. Once, a scattering of bird-shot pellets from a trespassing hunter. Though he was a coward, he had no discretion.

They'd also sprouted a number of cats, offspring of the single cat that had been transported to the farm from the city, and was supposed to have been spayed. Obviously there had been a mistake, because this cat kittened underneath a corner of the house. The kittens were quite wild. They ran away and plunged into their burrow if Nell even tried to get near them. Then they would peer out, hissing and trying to look ferocious. When they were older they moved to the barn, where they hunted mice and had secrets. Once in a while, a gizzard – squirrel, Nell suspected – or else a tail, or some other chewed-up body-part offering, would appear on the back-door threshold, where Nell would be sure to step on it, especially if her feet happened to be bare, as they often were in summer. The cats had a vestigial memory of civilization and its rituals, it seemed. They knew they were supposed to pay rent, but they were confused about the details.

They ate out of the dog's dish, which was kept outside the back door. Howl didn't bark at them or chase them: they were too terri-fying for him. Sometimes they slept on the cows. It was suspected that they had dealings in the hen house – eggshells had been found – but nothing could be proved.

The white horse – the white mare – had a name, unlike the cats. Her name was Gladys. She had been installed with Tig and Nell because of Nell's friend Billie, who was a horse-lover from child-hood but who lived in the city now, leaving her no outlets. Billie had seen the white horse (or mare) standing in a damp field, all by herself, hanging her head disconsolately. She was in a sad condition. Her mane was tangled, her white coat was muddy, and her hooves had not been dealt with for so long that her toes were turned up at the ends like Turkish slippers. Any more time in that swamp, said Billie, and she'd develop foot rot, and once a horse had that, it would soon go lame and that was pretty much game over. Billie had been so outraged by such callous neglect that she'd bought Gladys from a drunken and (she'd said) no doubt insane farmer, for a hundred dollars, which was a good deal more than poor Gladys was worth in her decrepit state.

But then Billie'd had no place to put her.

Nell and Tig had a place, however. They had lots of room – acres of it! What could be more perfect for Gladys (who was past her prime, who was too fat, who had something wrong with her wind so that she wheezed and coughed) than to come and stay at the farm? Just – of course – until something else could be found for her.

How could Nell say no? She could have said she had enough to do without adding a horse to her long, long list. She could have said she wasn't running a retirement home for rejected quadrupeds. But she hadn't wanted to sound selfish and cruel. Also, Billie was quite tall and determined, and had a convincing manner.

"I don't know anything about horses," Nell had said weakly. She didn't add that she was afraid of them. They were large and jumpy, and they rolled their eyes too much. She thought of them as unstable and prone to rages.

"Oh, it's easy. I'll teach you," said Billie. "There's nothing to it once you get the hang of it. You'll love Gladys! She has such a sweet nature! She's just a cupcake!"

When he heard about Gladys, Tig was reserved. He said that horses needed a lot of care. They also needed a lot of feed. But he'd accumulated all of the other animals – the ones that had been chosen and paid for, rather than just straying onto the property or being spawned on it or dumped on it – and Nell had had no say in those choices. She found herself defending the advent of Gladys as if she herself had made a deliberate and principled decision to take her in, even though she was already regretting her own slackness and lack of spine.

Gladys arrived in a rented horse car, and was backed out of it easily enough. "Come on, you old sweetie pie," Billie said. "There! Isn't she gorgeous?" Gladys turned around obediently and let herself be viewed. She had a round thick body, with legs that were too short for her bulk. She was part Welsh pit pony, part Arab, said Billie. That accounted for her odd shape. It also meant she would want to eat a lot. Welsh ponies were like that. Billie had made the trip in the horse car with her; she'd bought her a new bridle.

Nell was expected to pay for this bridle, and also for the horse-car rental: Gladys was now hers, it appeared. Surely that had not been the original understanding, but Billie thought it had been. She seemed to feel she was doing Nell a favour – had given her a priceless gift. She didn't charge for the original hundred dollars, nor for her own time. She'd taken a week off work to set Gladys up with Nell. She made a point of mentioning that.

Gladys regarded Nell through her long, frowsy forelock. She had the weary, blank, but calculating look of a carnival con artist: she was sizing Nell up, figuring her out, estimating how to get round her. Then she ducked her head and snatched at a tuft of grass.

"None of that, you naughty girl," said Billie, jerking Gladys's head up by the bridle. "You can't let them get away with anything," she told Nell. She led Gladys to the end of the drive shed, where there was a fenced-in space originally intended for goats – Nell had fought off the goat idea — and tied her up to one of the posts. "We'll put her in here for now," she said.

Billie volunteered to stay at the farm until Gladys was settled in, so Nell made up the recently acquired pullout couch in the former back parlour. The previous summer, Nell and Tig had tried to incubate some eggs in there, turning them and sprinkling them with water as per the instructions in the booklet that came with the incubator, but something went wrong and the chicks emerged with goggling eyes and swollen, blue-veined, unfinished stomachs, and had to be hit with a shovel and buried in the back field. Howl dug them up again, several times, after which the cats got into them, with unpleasant results. Nell kept finding tiny claws in unexpected places, as if the chicks were growing up through the barnyard dirt like disagreeable weeds.

Nell had taken to keeping tomato plants under a grow light in the back parlour, but she'd moved them to the upstairs landing in preparation for Billie's week-long stay.

Much had to be done for Gladys. Equipment was needed. Billie contributed some of her old horse things — a brush, a curry comb, a hoof pick — but the saddle had to be bought. It was second-hand, but still — thought Nell — breathtakingly expensive.

"You need the English, not the Western," Billie had said. "That way you'll learn to be a real rider." What she meant, it turned out, was that with the English saddle you had to grip with your knees or else you would fall off. Nell would rather have had the Western saddle — she had no interest in plummeting off a horse — but at least with Gladys it wasn't very far down to the ground, because of her stumpy little legs.

Saddle soap had to be applied to the saddle and worked in, metal items on the tackle had to be polished. A horse blanket was needed too, and a crop, and some old towels, for rubbing Gladys down. Gladys would have to be rubbed down like a boxer after every session of exercise, said Billie, because horses were delicate creatures, and the number of diseases or conditions they could get was staggering.

After the tackle had been brought up to scratch, Gladys herself had to be gone over, inch by inch. Nell did the work — because she had to learn how, didn't she? — with supervision by Billie. Dust and old hair came off Gladys in clouds, long white horsehairs from her mane and tail detached themselves and floated onto Nell. Gladys bore all this patiently, and might even have enjoyed it. Billie said she was enjoying it — she seemed to have a pipeline to Gladys's mind. She spent some time patiently explaining that mind to Nell so Nell wouldn't do anything that might spook Gladys and cause her to panic and bolt. The hens were a potential danger; so was the laundry. Nell had strung a clothesline between two of the apple trees out at the front of the house, which was therefore a no-go zone. "They hate flapping," Billie said. "They see a different picture out of each eye, so they don't like surprises. Life comes at them from all sides. It's unsettling for them. You can imagine."

A farrier was called in — luckily Billie knew one — and Gladys had her hooves trimmed, and sparkling new horseshoes applied. She was looking friskier now, she was taking more of an interest. Her ears swivelled around at the sound of Nell, who always had a carrot with her, or a sugar cube — this because of a hot tip from Billie.

"She has to bond with you," said Billie. "Breathe into her nose."

Then Nell had to try digging the stones out of Gladys's hooves. This needed to be done at least twice a day, said Billie, and also before riding Gladys, and after riding Gladys, because you never knew when she might pick up a stone. Nell was afraid of being kicked, but Gladys didn't mind having her feet picked out. "She knows it's for her own good," said Billie, whacking Gladys on the rump. "Don't you, you big lump?" Gladys was on a diet, despite the carrots. Being thinner — Billie claimed — would help with the wheezing problems. It would be necessary to ride Gladys every day: she needed the exercise, and also the excitement. Horses were easily bored, said Billie.

At last it was time to try Gladys out. The saddle was lifted onto her, the girths tightened. Gladys put her ears back and gave a crafty sideways look. Billie swung up into the saddle and kicked Gladys in the flanks, and Gladys cantered off down the road to the back field. They looked quite funny — top-heavy. Tall Billie astride fat Gladys, with Gladys's stumpy little legs whirring away underneath her like an eggbeater.

After a while Billie and Gladys came back. Gladys was wheezing, Billie pink in the face. "She's been ridden by too many people," said Billie. "She has a hard mouth. I bet she was used for kiddie rides."

"What do you mean?" said Nell.

"She has a whole bagful of tricks," said Billie. "Bad habits. She'll try them out on you, so look out."

"Tricks?"

"You just have to stay on," said Billie grimly, dismounting. "Once she knows you're on to her, she'll cut out the monkey business. You're a bad girl," she said to Gladys. Gladys coughed.

Nell found out what the tricks were the first time she tried to ride Gladys. Billie ran alongside, shouting instructions. "Don't let her get near the fence, she'll try to scrape you off! Keep her away from the trees! Don't let her stop, give her a kick! Pull her head up, she'd not allowed to eat that! Don't pay any attention to that cough, she's doing it on purpose!"

WHITE HORSE

Though Gladys wasn't going very fast, Nell clung on, resisting the impulse to lean forward and clutch Gladys by the mane. She had a vision of Gladys rearing up on her two back legs or else her two front legs, as in films, with the same result in either case – Nell shooting off into the bushes, headfirst. But nothing like that happened. At the end of the track, Gladys halted, wheezing and panting, and Nell actually got her to turn around. Then – after Gladys had glanced back over her shoulder with an incredulous but resigned stare – they repeated their odd merry-go-round motion, back to their starting point.

"Well done!" said Billie. "Good girl!" The praise was for Gladys. "See? You just have to be strict," she said to Nell.

When the week was over, Billie left, in a sullen mood, because Gladys had not been sufficiently grateful for having been rescued – she'd nipped Billie on the bum when having her head tied to a post as part of her diet procedure. Once Billie was no longer in the picture, Gladys and Nell came to an understanding. True, every time Nell approached with the bridle Gladys would start wheezing, but once the saddle was on she'd remember she might get a carrot at the end of her ordeal, and she would settle down, and off they would go, down to the back field – always the same track. They avoided the gravel side road – neither of them liked trucks – and the front of the house as well, because of the laundry; they didn't ride across the fields, because of hidden groundhog holes. During these rides Nell spent most of the time trying to make Gladys behave and the rest of it letting her do what she wanted, because Nell was curious about what that might be.

Sometimes Gladys wanted to stop in mid-canter to see if Nell would fall off. Sometimes she wanted to stand still, swishing her tail and sighing as if extremely tired. Sometimes she wanted to revolve slowly in a circle. Sometimes she wanted to eat weeds and wayside clover – Nell drew the line at that. Sometimes she wanted to go over to the barnyard fence and watch the sheep and cows, and also the cats, which had taken to sleeping on her broad, comfortable back.

Between the two of them, Nell and Gladys passed their riding time pleasantly enough. It was a conspiracy, a double imperson-ation: Nell pretending to be a person who was riding a horse, Gladys pretending to be a horse that was being ridden.

Sometimes they didn't bother cantering or trotting. They ambled along in the sunlight, lazily and without purpose. At these times Nell would talk to Gladys, which was better than talking to Howl, who was an idiot, or to the hens or cats. Gladys had to listen: she couldn't get away. "What do you think, Gladys?" Nell would say. "Should I have a baby?" Gladys, trudging along, sighing, would swivel an ear back in the direction of the voice. "Tig isn't sure. He says he isn't ready. Should I just do it? Would he get angry? Would it ruin everything? What do you think?"

Gladys would cough.

Nell would have preferred to have had this conversation with her mother, but her mother wasn't available. Anyway she probably wouldn't have said much more than Gladys. She too would have coughed, because she would have disapproved. Nell and Tig were – after all – not married. How could they possibly be married, when Tig couldn't manage to get himself divorced?

But if Nell's mother knew about Gladys, maybe she would come up to the farm. Her mother had been a devoted horse person once, a long time ago. She'd had two horses of her own. Was it conceivable that, with Gladys dangled like a lure in front of her, she might overcome her reservations – about Tig, about Nell, about their unorthodox living arrangements? Wouldn't she be tempted? Wouldn't she long to have one small idyllic canter out to the back field, for old times' sake, with Gladys's pony-sized legs going like an eggbeater? Wouldn't she want to know that Nell now loved – improbably, and at last – one of the same activities she herself had once loved?

Perhaps. But Nell had no way of knowing. She and her mother weren't exactly speaking. They weren't exactly not speaking, either. The silence that had taken the place of speech between them had become its own form of speech. In this silence, language was held suspended. It contained many questions, though no definite answers.

As spring turned into summer, Tig and Nell had more and more visitors, especially on the weekends. These visitors would just happen to be driving by, on a little outing from the city, and they'd drop in to say hello, and then they'd be invited for lunch – Tig loved cooking big impromptu lunches, featuring huge vats of soup and giant wads of cheese, and Nell's home-baked bread – and then the day would wear on and the visitors would stroll out to the back field for a walk. They were not allowed to ride Gladys, because of her bad manners with strangers, said Nell, though really she'd become possessive about her, she wanted to keep Gladys all to herself. Then Tig would say they might as well stay for dinner, and then it would be too dark or too late or they would be too drunk to drive back to the city, and they'd end up on the pullout couch in the back parlour, and – if there were a lot of them – dispersed here and there, some of them on foam mattresses or sofas.

In the mornings they would sit around after breakfast – stacks of Tig's wheat-germ pancakes were featured – saying how restful it was in the country, while Nell and Tig tidied up the dishes. They might stand around with their arms dangling at their sides, asking if there was anything they could do – Nell could remember when she herself was like that – and Nell might send them out to the hen-house with a basket padded with tea towels, to collect eggs, which gave them a thrill. Or she would put them to work weeding the garden. They would say how therapeutic it was to get dirt on their fingers; then they would breathe deeply as if they'd just discovered air; then they would have lunch again. After they'd left, Nell would wash their sheets and towels and hang them up on the outside line to flap in the sunshine between the apple trees.

Usually these visitors to the farm were couples, but Nell's baby sister, Lizzie, would come up by herself. The frequency of her visits was connected with the troubles in her life: if there were lots of troubles she would visit, if there weren't many troubles she wouldn't.

The troubles were about men, of which there had already been a number in her life. The men behaved badly. Nell listened to the accounts of their thoughtlessness, their contrariness, and their betrayals, coupled with descriptions of Lizzie's own shortcomings, flaws, and mistakes. She joined in the task of deciphering the men's casual remarks – remarks that usually had a mean and hurtful undertone, it was decided. Then Nell would take Lizzie's side and denounce the men as unworthy. At this point Lizzie would turn around and defend them. These men were exceptional – they were smart, talented, and sexy. In fact, they were perfect, except that they didn't love Lizzie enough. Nell sometimes wondered how much *enough* would be.

Lizzie had been born when Nell was eleven. She'd been an anxious baby and then an anxious child and then an anxious teenager, but now she was twenty-three. Nell hoped the anxiety would begin to wear off soon.

WHITE HORSE

It was her anxiety that caused Lizzie to pick away at the men, peeling them down through their callous and blemished outer layers to get at their pristine cores — at the good, kind hearts she believed were hidden inside them somewhere, like truffles or oil wells. The men didn't seem to relish the process of being peeled, not in the long run. But no one could stop Lizzie from doing it. This would go on until some other man would come along, and then the former man would be archived.

Lizzie and Nell had the same noses. They both bit their fingers. Other than that, there were differences. Nell looked the age she was, but Lizzie could have been mistaken for a fourteen-year-old. She was thin, delicate-looking, with big eyes the colour of blue-green hydrangeas. Hydrangeas were a flower she favoured; she had a list of other favourite flowers. She liked the ones with small petals.

She thought Nell and Tig should plant some hydrangeas at the farm. She had other planting suggestions as well.

Lizzie loved the farm. Certain of its aspects enraptured her — the apple blossoms, the wild plum trees along the fencelines, the swallows dipping over the pond. One beautiful day, Nell and Lizzie were sitting outside the back door making ice cream. The inner ice cream canister was turned by electricity; they'd run an extension cord into the house. The outer canister was packed with chipped ice and rock salt. Some of the cats were watching from a distance: they knew there was cream involved. Howl had been over to investigate but had been alarmed by the whirring noise the machine was making and had backed away, whimpering.

As for Gladys, she was keeping an eye on them from the other side of the barnyard fence. She lived inside the barnyard now, because Nell had decided the sheep and cows would be company for her. After a short period of terrorizing the sheep by stampeding them around the barnyard, teeth bared, tail fully erect, she'd turned them into a herd of what she must have decided were dwarfish, woolly horses, and now bossed them around. They in turn had accepted her as a giant balding sheep, and followed her everywhere. She dealt with the cows and their lumbering attempts to monopolize the food supply by sneaking up on them and biting them; Nell had even witnessed a kick. These activities and the chance they gave her to express herself had improved her frame of mind immeasurably. She was now quite perky, like a housebound drudge recently widowed and in the process of discovering the pleasures of nail polish, hair salons, and bingo. Her diet was a thing of the past, Nell having been proven too feeble to enforce it.

"Isn't this *normal?*" said Nell, meaning the ice cream, the cats, the dog, Gladys looking over the fence – the whole bucolic scene. What she meant was *domestic.*

"This air's so great," said Lizzie, breathing in. "You should stay here forever. You shouldn't even bother going in to the city. When are you going to get rid of that rusty old machinery?"

"It's lawn sculpture. That would suit *them*," said Nell. "They'd never have to see me again."

"They'll get over it," said Lizzie. "Anyway they live in the Middle Ages. Is it a harrow?"

"They might like Gladys," said Nell hopefully.

"Gladys is beside the point," said Lizzie.

Nell thought about that. "Not to herself," she said. "I think it's actually a disker. The other one's a drag harrow."

"They wouldn't like Howl," said Lizzie. "He's too craven for them. What you need is a rusty old car."

WHITE HORSE

"We've got one, we're driving it," said Nell. "He's mentally deficient. I can see their point though. Everything's different now. They aren't used to it."

"That's their problem," said Lizzie, who despite her fragility could be tough when it came to other people, and especially other people who were doing wounding things to Nell.

When Lizzie and Nell spoke together, they often left out the middle terms of thought sequences because they knew the other one would fill them in. *Them* meant their parents, in whose books – outdated, prudish books, according to Lizzie – only cheap, trashy women did things like living with married men.

Lizzie was the messenger. She took it as her mission to assure their parents that Nell was not dying of any fatal disease, and to report to Nell that it was not yet time for the parents to meet Tig, of whom Lizzie approved, with reservations. First the parents would have to enter the twentieth century. Lizzie herself would be the judge of when that had happened.

It's fun for her to be the judge, thought Nell. She's been on the judged end enough times. She probably has discussions with them about me. Me and my bad behaviour. Now I'm the problem child, for a change.

"How's Claude?" she said. Claude was Lizzie's current man. He'd been away a lot, on trips, and had been offhand about his dates of return. He was away right now, and a week overdue.

"There's something wrong with my digestive system," said Lizzie. What she meant was, I am feeling very anxious, because of Claude. "I think I have irritable bowel syndrome. I have to see a doctor about it."

"He just needs to grow up," said Nell.

"I mean, he might be dead or something," said Lizzie. "He doesn't get that part."

"What are you talking about?" said Tig, coming around the corner of the house. "Is the ice cream ready?"

"You," said Nell.

Lizzie came up the next weekend. "What about your irritable bowel syndrome?" Nell asked her.

"The doctor couldn't find anything," Lizzie said. "He referred me to a shrink. He thinks it's psychological."

Nell didn't think this was a totally bad idea. Maybe the shrink could do something about the anxiety, the crises, the troubles with men. Help Lizzie get some perspective.

"Are you going to go?" she asked. "To the shrink?"

"I've already been," said Lizzie.

A few weeks later, Lizzie came up again. She didn't say much and seemed preoccupied. It was hard to wake her in the mornings. She was tired at lot of the time.

"The shrink's put me on a pill," she said. "It's supposed to help the anxiety."

"And has it?" said Nell.

"I'm not sure," said Lizzie.

She hadn't been to see their parents lately, she said. She hadn't got around to it. She no longer seemed to care what the parents thought of Nell and her immoral lifestyle, a subject that had once been of much interest to her.

Claude had departed, possibly for good. Lizzie expressed anger with him, but in a curiously detached way. There was no new man on the scene. She didn't seem to care about that, either. She appeared to have shelved the plans she'd had – just a few weeks earlier – for going back to school in the fall. She'd been quite excited about it then, and hopeful. It was going to be a whole new chapter.

Nell was concerned, but decided to wait and see.

The weekend after that Lizzie was back again. She was walking stiffly and drooling a little. Her face lacked expression. She said she felt weak. Also she'd quit her temporary job, which had been in a sportswear store.

"There's something really wrong with Lizzie," Nell said to Tig. She wondered if some malign influence in the back parlour – the same influence that had wreaked such havoc with the incubating chicks – was affecting Lizzie. The neighbourhood farmers had let it drop, almost casually, that the farmhouse was haunted: that was why it had been on the market for so long before Tig and Nell had bought it, as everyone with any sense had always known.

Nell didn't entirely believe in this haunting phenomenon and had seen no direct evidence of it. Still, Howl the dog wouldn't go into that room, and sometimes barked at it. But this in itself proved nothing, as his phobias were numerous. Mrs. Roblin from up the road said some kids had once stolen a marble tombstone from the cemetery and used it for making pull taffy in that house, which had been a bad idea: the ghost might have got in that way. Mrs. Roblin was considered to be an authority on such matters: she always took care never to have thirteen to dinner, and was said to be able to smell blood on the stairs whenever there was to be a violent death – a car crash, a lightning strike, a tractor rolling over and squashing its driver.

Mrs. Roblin had told Nell to leave a meal on the table overnight, to let the ghost know it was welcome. (Nell, feeling foolish, had actually done this, in the middle of the previous winter, during a blizzard, when things had got a little too dark and foreboding. A slice of ham and some mashed potatoes were what she thought such a spirit might like. But Howl had snuck in somehow and eaten this food offering, and tipped over the glass of milk Nell had placed beside it, so leaving out the meal might not have accomplished much.)

Could the rumoured haunting entity have got into Lizzie? But such a thought was ridiculous. Anyway, now that it was summer, the house did not seem very haunted after all.

"It must be the pills," said Tig.

Neither of them knew much about pills. Nell decided to phone the shrink, whose name was Dr. Hobbs. She left a message with the secretary. After a few days, Dr. Hobbs phoned back.

The conversation was very disturbing.

Dr. Hobbs said that Lizzie was a schizophrenic, and that he had therefore put her on an antipsychotic drug. That would control the symptoms of her mental illness, which were many. He himself would see her once a week, though she would have to call ahead to set the time, as he was very busy and he would have to make a special effort to fit her in. Lizzie could drive into the city for these sessions, which would deal with her inability to adjust to real life. Meanwhile, said Dr. Hobbs, Lizzie would be incapable of holding down a job, going to school, or functioning independently. She would have to live with Nell and Tig.

Why not with Nell's parents? Nell asked, once she had caught her breath.

"It's her preference to live with you," said Dr. Hobbs.

Nell knew nothing about schizophrenia. Lizzie hadn't ever seemed crazy to Nell, just sometimes very sorrowful and despondent, but maybe that was because Nell was used to her. She remembered that she and Lizzie had some odd uncles, so it might be genetic. But then, everyone had odd uncles. Or a lot of people did.

"How do you know Lizzie's a schizophrenic?" Nell said. She wanted to sit down – she felt sick to her stomach – but the telephone was on the wall and the cord was too short.

Dr. Hobbs laughed in a condescending way. *I'm the professional*, his tone said. "It's the word salad," he said.

"What is word salad?" said Nell.

"She doesn't make any sense when she talks," said the doctor. Nell had never noticed this.

"Are you sure?" she said.

"Sure about what?" said Dr. Hobbs.

"That she's – what you say she is."

The doctor laughed again. "If she wasn't a schizophrenic, these drugs she's on would kill her," he said. He then said that Nell should not say anything to Lizzie about the diagnosis. That was a delicate matter, and needed to be handled with care.

Nell called him back the next week. She had trouble getting through – she left several messages – but she persisted, because Lizzie's state was becoming more and more alarming. "What about the way she's walking?" she asked. Lizzie's hands were beginning to shake, she'd noticed. Dr. Hobbs said that the stiffness and the drooling and shaking were symptoms of Lizzie's disease—all schizophrenics had those symptoms. Lizzie was just the age at which this disease manifested itself. A person could seem perfectly normal, and then in their late teens or early twenties, out came the schizophrenia, like some malignant blossom.

"How long is this going to go on?" said Nell.

"The rest of her life," said Dr. Hobbs.

Nell felt cold all over. Though Lizzie'd had some bad times in the past, Nell had never suspected anything like this.

She discussed the situation with Tig after Lizzie had gone to bed. How would he feel, being saddled with a mad relative?

"We'll cope," he said. "Maybe she'll snap out of it." Nell felt so grateful to him she almost wept.

There were a lot of other things Nell needed to know over the next few months. How could Lizzie be trusted with driving a car — Tig's old Chevy — back and forth to the city, with her body so stiff and her hands shaking like that? But Dr. Hobbs — whose tone was becoming more and more hostile, as if he felt Nell was pestering him — said that was fine, Lizzie was perfectly capable of driving.

He also said he hadn't told Lizzie the truth about her condition yet because she wasn't ready for that news. She was hallucinating about some man called Claude, he said; she was convinced Claude was dead. Also she'd been suicidal when she'd come to him. But he could guarantee that she wouldn't commit suicide any time soon.

"Why not?" said Nell. She'd thought that *I'm going to kill myself* was a figure of speech for Lizzie, as it was for her. Now it appeared she'd been wrong; nevertheless she felt preternaturally calm. She was getting used to these fragments of nightmare that kept coming at her out of the mouth of Dr. Hobbs.

But Dr. Hobbs appeared to be confused about who she was: he seemed to think that she and Tig were Lizzie's parents. Nell carefully explained the actual relationship, but every time she spoke with him she had to remind him about it.

Meanwhile, Lizzie's real parents — Nell's parents — had gone into shock. But they were talking to Nell again, or at least her mother was. "I don't know what to do," she would say. It was a plea — *Don't send her back here!* It was as if Lizzie had committed some shameful, unmentionable act — something in between a social gaffe and a crime.

Then Nell's mother would ask plaintively, "When is she going to get better?" As if Nell had any special insights.

"I'm sure the doctor knows what's right," Nell would say. She still believed that anyone with a medical degree must know what he was talking about. She needed to believe that: she put some effort into it. "You should come up to the farm and see my horse," she added. "You like horses. Her name is Gladys. You could go for a ride." But her mother was too distressed by Lizzie's plight.

Nell herself hadn't been riding Gladys much, because she was pregnant. She didn't want to be thrown off a horse and lose the baby, as happened in novels. She hadn't yet shared her knowledge with Tig, however.

What would it be like if the baby arrived and Lizzie was still like this? How could she manage?

By now it was September. Nell tried to get Lizzie to help her with the preserving, but it was no use: Lizzie was too tired. Nell set a bowl of red currants in front of her and asked her to pick off the stems — that wouldn't be too hard — but Lizzie couldn't seem to manage it. She sat at the table, gazing into space, with her pathetic little mound of picked-over currants shoved to one side.

"He doesn't like me," she said. "The doctor."

"Why wouldn't he like you?" said Nell.

"Because I'm not getting better," said Lizzie.

Tig had been doing some research of his own. "This guy isn't making any sense," he said. "Those pills won't kill you if you aren't schizophrenic — how could they? You'd have a lot of corpses to explain."

"But why would he tell us that?" said Nell.

"Because he's a fraud," said Tig.

"I think we need a second opinion," said Nell.

. . .

The new doctor they found was an expert in antipsychotic drugs. "Lizzie shouldn't have been put on this," she told Nell. "I'm taking her off it." The stiffness, the trembling, the weakness — all those were by no means the symptoms of a disease. They were produced by the drug itself, and once the stuff was out of Lizzie's system they would go away.

Not only that, Lizzie should never have been allowed to drive a car while so heavily medicated, said the new doctor. Her life had been in danger every minute she'd been behind the wheel.

"If I ever met that creep on the street I'd shoot him," Nell said to Tig. "If I had a gun."

"Lucky you don't know what he looks like," said Tig.

"I bet he thought we were hillbillies," said Nell. "Because we live on a farm. I bet he thought he could tell us any old thing, and we'd believe it." Which had in fact been the case, they had believed it. "He must've thought we were dumb as a sack of hammers. I wonder if he believed any of it himself? If so, he's a lunatic!"

"Hillbillies?" said Tig. "Where did you dig up *that* word? Though we've got the farm machinery for it!" Then they both started to laugh, and hugged each other, and Nell told him about the baby, and it was all fine.

Nell felt tremendous relief at the new turn of events — she wouldn't have to look after a drooling, shambling Lizzie for the rest of her life — but she also felt a shiver of fear. Lizzie would not go back to being the way she was before Dr. Hobbs got hold of her: her interlude as a zombie would have changed her. She would now be someone else, someone as yet unknown. Also, Nell was well aware that Lizzie would consider her own actions a betrayal. And Lizzie would be right – they were a betrayal. If Nell had been the supposed schizophrenic, Lizzie wouldn't have put up with Dr. Hobbs and his toxic gobbledegook for two seconds.

"Why didn't you tell me what he thought?" Lizzie said to Nell, once she was no longer tranquilized. Now, instead, she was furious. "You should have asked me! I could have told you I wasn't a schizophrenic!"

Useless for Nell to say that once you think someone's unhinged you don't trust their word, especially on the subject of their own mental health. So she didn't say it.

"He told me you had word salad," Nell said weakly.

"He told you I had what?"

"He said you didn't make sense."

"Oh for fuck's sake! I talked to him the same way I talk to you!" said Lizzie. "We skip the middles of sentences, you know that. He just had trouble *following* me. He couldn't get from A to C! I had to spell things out for him. He was just plain, ordinary stupid!"

"He must have been having a nervous breakdown, or something," said Nell. "To be so – so unprofessional." And malevolent, she felt like adding. It was Tig's opinion that Dr. Hobbs had been doing secret drug experiments for the CIA, an idea that had seemed far-fetched, at the time.

"Well, he's fucked up my life," said Lizzie grimly. "I've *lost* a big chunk of it. What an asshole!"

"Not that much," said Nell soothingly. She meant the big chunk of life.

"Fine for you to say," said Lizzie. "You weren't there."

. . .

It was decided that Lizzie would stay on at the farm until some plan could be formulated. For one thing, she didn't have any money. It was too late for her to go back to school this year, as she'd intended doing before the catastrophe of Dr. Hobbs.

She was seeing her new doctor once a week. The subject was family issues. She went for long walks around the farm, and dug vigorous holes in the garden. She wasn't saying much to Tig and Nell, though she made friends with Gladys. She didn't ride her, but she would run around in the barnyard with her, the cows moving aside to let them past, the sheep following behind. Her lassitude of the summer had been replaced by a ferocious energy.

Nell, who was now swelling visibly, watched through the window, a little envious: she wouldn't be able to gallop around like that for a while. Then she went back to kneading the bread, letting herself settle into the soft curves, the soothing warmth, the peaceful rhythm. She thought they were all out of danger now; she thought Lizzie was.

Then, one crisp October night, Lizzie attached the vacuum cleaner hose to the exhaust pipe of the car, ran it in through the window, and turned on the motor.

Tig heard the motor running and went outside. By the time he got to her, he said, Lizzie had turned the motor off and was just sitting there. He said this was a good sign. He'd had to wake Nell up to tell her this. How could she have been asleep at such a time?

After getting herself under control, Nell came downstairs in her nightgown, with an old sweater of Tig's thrown on top of it. She felt cold all over. Her teeth were chattering.

By then Lizzie and Tig were sitting at the kitchen table having hot chocolate. "Why did you do that?" Nell said to Lizzie, once she could speak. She was trembling with fright, and with what she would much later come to discover had been rage.

"I don't want to discuss it," said Lizzie.

"No. I mean, why did you do that, *to me?*"

"You'd cope with it," said Lizzie. "You cope with everything."

It wasn't the same night that Gladys ran away, but Nell remembers it as the same night. She can't seem to separate the two events. She remembers Howl barking, though it's unlikely he would have done anything so appropriate. She also remembers a full moon – a chilly, white, autumnal moon – another atmospheric detail she herself may well have supplied. But a full moon would have been fitting, because animals are more active then.

It was the cows who'd set the tragedy in motion, on one of their periodic jailbreaks. They'd got the fence down again and had taken off for the nearest herd of other cows. Gladys, on the other hand, had made for the paved highway two miles away. She must have been bored with her little kingdom, she must have been tired of ruling over the sheep. Also, Nell hadn't been paying enough attention to her. She'd wanted an adventure.

She was hit by a car and killed. The driver had been drinking, and was going fast. It must have been a shock to him to have flown over the top of the hill and seen a white horse standing right in front of him, lit up by the moonlight. He himself was only shaken, but his car was a mess.

Nell felt terrible about Gladys. She felt guilty and sad. But she didn't want to indulge these feelings because they would cause upsetting chemicals to circulate through her bloodstream, and that might affect the baby. She listened to a lot of Mozart string quartets in an attempt to stay cheerful.

The next fall she planted a patch of daffodils at the front of the property, in memory of Gladys. The daffodils came up every year, and grew well, and spread.

They are still there. Nell knows that, because she drove past the farm a few years ago just to see it again. When was that, exactly? Shortly after Lizzie got married, and went in for home cooking, and gave up sorrow. Whenever it was, it was in the spring, and there were the daffodils, hundreds of them by now.

The farmhouse itself had lost its ramshackle appearance. It looked serene and welcoming, and somewhat suburban. Laundry no longer flapped between the apple trees. The rusting farm machinery had gone. The siding on the house had been freshly painted, a fashionable colour of pioneer blue. On either side of the front door was a planter with a shrub in it – rhododendrons, thought Nell. Whoever was living there now preferred things tidier.

The Entities

L illie was a real-estate agent, though she was hardly the image of one. There was nothing sharp-edged or chic or brisk about her, and she was twenty years older than the oldest real-estate agent that she herself had met. Her car – a white car, a Ford sedan, always impeccably clean – was not a recent model. She drove it cautiously, peering over the top of the steering wheel like someone in a tank turret.

She was getting plump, and her feet were beginning to hurt; she wheezed a little going up and down stairs. Despite these hindrances, she went up and down the stairs of every house she showed. "Feh," she'd say, sidestepping down to the basement. "Don't look, it's just their laundry. The furnace – you can get new. You'll redo the wiring, we'll get a couple thousand off the price minimum, at least it's dry." She'd clamber up the stairs to the attic, pausing to breathe, and to inspect the cracks in the plaster. "You'll put in a skylight, you'll knock out the walls, listen, it'll be a space. Don't look in there, it's junk. The wallpaper — it's only wallpaper, you know what I mean?"

She'd say, "The way some peoples live — like pigs! These are not nice peoples. But you'll make it new — a different house, you wouldn't recognize it!" She believed this — that with a little effort and a lot of faith a pig pen could be transformed into something wonderful, or at least something habitable. Something a lot better than it had been before.

She specialized in smaller houses on neglected streets, downtown — old Victorian row houses or dark, narrow semi-detached brick boxes, owned by Portuguese families who'd stuck wrought-iron porch railings onto them, and before that by Russians or Hungarians, and before that by who knows? These neighbourhoods were stopovers — people lived in them right after they got off the boat, before they made good and moved on. That was the way it had been once. Now, young couples were seeking out such places — such cheap places. Artistic people were seeking them out.

Such people — Lillie said *pipples* — such people needed someone to take them by the hand, help them buy at a decent price, because they weren't practical, they didn't know from furnaces, the sellers would take advantage. Lillie would haggle the price down even though it made her own commission smaller, because what was money? When the deal was signed she'd present the young artists with a celebration gift, a bowl filled with cookies she'd made herself — hard, beige, European cookies — and then she would follow the transformation of the house as the artistic youngsters set to work. These people had such energy, they had their own ideas; it was a joy to watch them ripping off the dour wallpaper and doing away with the mildew and the lingering smells and stains of the past and then building something else – a studio, they would always need such a thing, if there was a garage they'd use that – and then painting the walls, not the colours she herself would have chosen, often a little startling, but she liked surprises of a certain kind. Good surprises. "You never know," she'd say. Such a pleasure.

Not that she herself would have taken on a house like that. Such houses were too cramped, too dim, too old. She had a modern house, farther north, with big light-filled windows and a collection of pastel-tinted china figurines, and a wide driveway.

Lillie had come to the real-estate business late in life. Long ago she'd been a young girl, and then she'd married, a fine man, and then she'd had a baby; all of that was in another time, on the other side of the ocean. But after that came the Nazis, and she'd been put into a camp and her husband had been put into a different one, and the baby was lost and never found again. But Lillie had made it through, not like most, and miraculously she'd located her husband after the war was over, he'd made it through as well, it was a blessing; and after that they'd had two more babies, and then they'd moved to Canada, to Toronto, where a person did not have to be reminded. Such a name for a city, Toronto – it had an Italian sound, though it wasn't an Italian word at all, and the winters could be long; but a person could get used to it, and Lillie had.

The babies grew up, they were fine children, you couldn't ask for better, they spoiled her, and then the husband died. Lillie didn't speak of him, but she kept his suits in the closet; she couldn't bear to give them away. Dead was not an absolute concept to her. Some people were more dead than others, and finally it was a matter of opinion who was dead and who was alive, so it was best not to discuss such a thing. Similarly she did not speak of the camp she'd been put into, nor of the lost baby. Why speak? What difference would it make? Who'd want to hear? Anyway she'd been luckier than most. She'd been so lucky.

She encouraged her young couples, and listened to their problems, and cheered them up and told them who to call when they got downcast about clogged drains or dry rot or carpenter ants, and protected them from faulty wiring. She took an interest in their children, if any, and their divorces, if any. She kept in touch. When it was time for them to sell and buy something else — move up the ladder, get maybe a bigger studio — she was always the person they consulted.

She wouldn't go to the house-warming parties, though. She couldn't manage parties. They made her feel sad. She'd send her bowl of cookies, with a nice note on flowered notepaper. They deserved such a house, she would write. They were good people. They should enjoy it. She was happy for them. She wished them well.

When Nell and Tig were planning to move in from the country, they inherited Lillie from a friend. Lillie got passed around from one youngish couple to the next. "She won't try to sell you anything you can't afford," was the word. "You can tell her exactly what you want. She'll get the idea."

At their first meeting, Nell found herself running off at the mouth to Lillie. It was Lillie's pleasant face, her air of reassurance. Much as they'd loved the farm, Nell said, generalizing slightly, they really needed to move, it was time, they'd been there too long, things had changed, the old families had gone, all the people they knew. Here Lillie nodded. Not only that, but there'd been too many break-ins, a house almost across the road – a retired schoolteacher – had been totally cleaned out by two men with a moving van. You couldn't feel safe.

"These are not nice peoples," said Lillie.

"They watch your house," said Nell. "They know when you're away." And anyway, Nell and Tig had a nearly school-age child who'd have to spend two hours on a bus every day, and anyway the house was dark somehow, the locals said it was haunted, not that Nell personally had ever seen anything but there was a feeling, and anyway it was cold in winter, it was a hundred and fifty years old, it had never been properly insulated, snow piled up on the driveway.

"This you don't need," said Lillie. She had a man shovel her driveway. It was always kept clear. You needed to live in a city to have a man who shovelled.

And Tig hadn't been as well as he might have been, said Nell. It was the lack of insulation, he got coughs, it had all become too much for Nell, she couldn't cope. "The cows escape," she said. "They want to be with other cows. Then if Tig isn't there, it's only me."

Lillie nodded, she understood: a young and busy mother like Nell could not be expected to deal with escaping cows. "You shouldn't worry," she said, "we'll find perfect," and Nell felt immediately better. Lillie would take care of things.

The housing market was hot right then but Lillie did her best, and Nell and Tig ended up in a fairly good row house near the art gallery, on the edge of Chinatown. The house was already renovated, so it was all right, better than all right under the circumstances, the circumstances being financial: this house was something they could manage. It was quite nice really, except that the cockroaches came in from the houses on either side. Nell put cucumber peels and Borax along the baseboards: there was no point in fumigating, because apart from the toxicity the cockroaches would just seep back in once the effects had worn off.

After a couple of years of that house, Lillie decided it was time for Nell and Tig to move again. "You need bigger," she told them, and she was right. She sold their house for a good price and shifted them farther north. The orange shag carpeting left over from the 1970s was only carpet, she said, when showing them the house. They shouldn't look at the plate racks everywhere, those could go, and never mind the light fixtures. There were three fireplaces, a fireplace was not junk, and the walls were solid, the house had spacious that lots of peoples would kill for, and some of the woodwork was original, such details counted for a lot.

Nell and Tig were pleased: now they'd have a back garden, and a basement that was finished — well, half-finished, and the mouldy indoor-outdoor glued to the cement floor could come off — and windows all around: in the row house, the windows were confined to the front and the back. On the day the deal closed, Lillie gave them a blue and orange bowl full of her own cookies.

When Nell found she had a problem — an unusual problem, she felt — Lillie was the only person she could talk to about it. It was a problem with houses, but it was also a problem with human nature. It wasn't a thing she could discuss with Tig — he got too anxious, and some of the human nature in question was his. But Lillie must have seen a lot of cellars and attics and human nature in her day. She must know that houses were powerful, that people could get stirred up about them, that they could bring out feelings you wouldn't expect. Nothing Nell could tell her would shock or dismay her: she'd seen it all — surely — before. Or something like it. Or worse.

THE ENTITIES

Nell asked Lillie over to tea. Tea was about the only thing in the form of eats and drinks that Lillie could be persuaded to share: she would never come to dinner. Nell served up some of Lillie's severe cookies — they kept almost indefinitely — to show that she appreciated them; which she did, though not as cookies, exactly.

Nell and Lillie had their tea in Nell's recently acquired kitchen. "Such a view," said Lillie, gazing out over the back garden.

Nell agreed. For both of them it was a view of the future: there was nothing in the garden at present except some wispy grass, a corrugated tin shed, and a number of holes in the ground. The people before — they of the plate racks and shag carpets — had had a dog. But Nell planned great things — daffodils, anyway — when she could get around to it. One of her New Age friends who did feng shui and sageing had gone over the garden, and the house as well, with a view to orientation and psychic entities, and had pronounced the place benign, especially the garden, so Nell had no doubt that things could be made to flourish there.

"I thought maybe some daffodils," said Nell.

"Daffodils are good," said Lillie.

"To begin with," said Nell.

Lillie dipped her cookie into her tea. Aha, thought Nell, that's what you're supposed to do with them. "So," said Lillie, glancing at Nell obliquely, raising her eyebrows. That meant: You didn't ask me here to look at a field.

"Oona wants a house," Nell said.

"Lots of peoples want a house," said Lillie placidly.

"But this is Oona."

"So?" said Lillie. She knew who Oona was: she was Tig's first wife. First wives, second wives — an old story.

"She wants me to buy the house, so she can live in it."

Lillie's teacup paused in the air. "She said it?" This was something new.

"Not out loud," said Nell. "Not to me. But I know."

Lillie took another cookie and dipped it into her tea, and settled herself to listen.

The fact was that Oona was falling apart, said Nell. When they'd first met, Oona had been a force. Not only had she been attractive – in a voluptuous way, Nell thought to herself, with disapproval – but she'd had a strong will and strong opinions and the determination to get what she wanted. Or that had been what most people were allowed to see. True, she'd fall into depressions, but during those times she went to bed, so people didn't see this side of Oona. They saw only the bright, steady, somewhat mocking face she turned outward. She was known for her efficiency, for being up to challenges, for getting things done. She worked as a manager. She was employed by small concerns – small magazines, small theatre companies – small, failing magazines and theatre companies – and she rearranged their systems and whipped them into shape.

When Tig had moved out, their wider circle had been surprised. Everything had seemed so calm. It was well known that the two of them had had an understanding, and that Oona in particular had gone through a series of male companions, but the situation itself had appeared stable. The rage – valid on both sides, Nell added fairly, because it always takes two, doesn't it? – that rage had been buried; but like so many buried things it had refused to stay under the ground forever.

After the breakup, Oona spread a message of contentment. She was the one who'd asked Tig to leave: it seemed better that way. The children were fine; they would spend weekends and vacations with Tig, in the country. She herself had needed more freedom from constriction, more space, more time to herself. More scope. That was the word from Oona, for the first year.

The addition of Nell as a fixture in Tig's life had been taken in stride by Oona – why not, since it had been partly her doing? She'd introduced Tig and Nell, she'd facilitated their – what would you call it? Their thing. "Tig and his harem," she'd say. "Of course, Nell is very young." Her expression said: *young and dumb*. The implication was that Nell would be temporary: Nell would leave Tig because he was too elderly, or Tig would leave Nell because she was too shallow. If the two of them wanted to fester away in that rented shack out in the sticks with the falling-down barn and the weeds – here Oona would smile and shrug – well, good luck to them. It would drive most people mad, herself included. In the meantime, the children enjoyed the country, at intervals, and Oona herself had more scope, the scope she'd always wanted.

She would make use of this scope at the last minute. Something would come up – some chance of an outing with the current companion. Then she would phone Nell and issue instructions: when the children were to be picked up, when they were to be delivered back, what they should eat. Her tone was cordial, even faintly amused. What could Nell say, standing on the slanting floor in the drafty farm kitchen, but Yes and Yes?

"Yes ma'am, is what she wants," said Nell to her friends. "She treats me like the hired help." That was Nell's view, though she couldn't get Tig to see it. Whenever it was a question of the children, Tig's eyes glazed over and he turned into a kind of robot. So it was the best method – said Nell – just to bite her tongue and not say anything.

Not that she had practised this method very rigorously. But she'd tried.

"Such a good father," said Lillie. "He wants the best for his children."

"I know," said Nell.

"A child — that comes first," said Lillie.

"I know," said Nell. She did know, too, now that she had one herself. But all this had happened some years before.

So that was the way things went, said Nell, for the first year or so. Then Nell and Tig had stopped renting and had bought a farm of their own, one that was less decrepit; though not much less, because they hadn't had very much money.

But Oona assumed there was a lot more money than there really was, Nell told Lillie. She demanded more from Tig — for the children — than she'd been getting. But if Tig had given her any more, said Nell, they wouldn't have been able to meet their own mortgage payments. As it was, half their living expenses were being covered by Nell. More than half. Not that Nell held it against Tig. But two and two did not make five.

Arithmetic made no difference to Oona. She began telling mutual acquaintances back in the city what an awful person Nell was, and how she had turned Tig into an awful person as well. Nell heard about these remarks, as Oona intended she should: people were never shy about repeating such things.

Oona changed lawyers — Tig and Oona were drawing up the divorce settlement by then — and when the new lawyer couldn't squeeze any more cash out of Tig, she changed lawyers again.

"He didn't have any more money," said Nell. "What could he do? You can't get blood from a stone."

"But you had it," said Lillie.

"Not really," said Nell. "She wrote some pretty vicious letters to Tig. By that time she was acting as if he'd abandoned her – like some Victorian scoundrel. Tig wouldn't say a bad word about her though, because of the kids."

"She was the mother," said Lillie. "When it's the mother and it's boys, that's the end of it."

"In a nutshell," said Nell. Lillie looked puzzled, so she added, "Exactly."

Still, the new farm was no mansion, as the boys duly reported to Oona – there were rats, for one thing, and in the spring the dirt-floor cellar filled with water, and in the winter the wind blew right through the walls – so in time Oona calmed down somewhat. She went on vacations with the various companions, to semi-tropical locations, but though Tig hoped one of the companions would became a permanent installation, none did.

Time passed, and Tig and Nell moved back into the city – into the row house in Chinatown, the one with the cockroaches, which wasn't much of a threat to Oona. The boys were grown up by now; they were no longer living with Oona. Tig could make his own arrangements with them, he didn't have to go through Oona. So that source of friction was removed. Nell felt lighter, and less muted.

But then two things happened. Oona was forced to leave her large, convenient apartment and found herself in a series of un-satisfactory sublets, just at the point when she'd quit her latest job; and Tig and Nell moved to their new house, the house that she and Lillie were sitting in right now, having their tea.

"She can't stand it," said Nell. "She thinks we're living in a palace. We were just lucky, we bought and sold at the right times, but she thinks we're rolling in cash. It's driving her up the wall."

"You can see it," said Lillie. "This happens. But she is a grown-up. Some have, some don't have."

"Yes," said Nell. "But also she's not well."

Oona's illness had been creeping up on her for years. She'd put on a lot of weight, and as she'd gained flesh she'd lost substance. Also she'd lost her nerve. The assurance that had carried her through was evaporating: she'd become hesitant, insecure. She was afraid of things. She didn't want to go out of the house, or into any kind of tunnel, such as the subway.

Oona had been to doctor after doctor: none of them could cast any light on her condition. It might be this, it might be that. Every once in a while she'd collapse – right on the sidewalk, the latest time – and then she'd be carted off to the hospital and given yet another medication that didn't work. Right now she was in a place with noisy neighbours who shouted and threw parties at night; in the mornings, needles would be found on the lawn. It was difficult and squalid, and frightening to Oona. That Oona could be so genuinely frightened was a new concept for Nell.

Tig said that if he had the money he would buy Oona a house to live in, for the sake of the boys. He said it into the air, not looking at Nell. He said that the boys were very worried.

Tig in his turn was worried about the boys, leaving Nell to be worried about Tig.

"They are good boys," said Lillie, who'd met them. "Such nice manners. They want to help their mother."

"I know," said Nell. "Oona and the boys both think she'd be better off in her own house, without any other tenants. It would be quieter. But she can't afford it."

"And Tig — what does he think?"

"Tig won't discuss it."

Lillie gave Nell a shrewd look. "What can you do?" she said.

Nell knew what she could do. She'd had a windfall, a little inheritance, not much, but enough. She'd stowed it away in the bank, in a safe investment. It sat there accusingly, and was not mentioned.

Lillie helped Nell find the house. The real-estate market was a white-hot feeding frenzy right then, properties were flipping so fast it made a person dizzy, said Lillie, so it wasn't easy. Better Oona should have wanted a house when it was a buyers' market, but life was life. Not only that, Oona had a list of requirements: no poor areas, she was terrified of being poor. Not too dark. Not too many stairs. A streetcar stop nearby. A store she could walk to. A garden.

At first Lillie drove Oona around, always with one of the boys; but as she reported back to Nell, it was no use. "She wants a castle," she said. "The boys tell her such houses are too big. They are suffering, these boys, they want that their mother should be happy, they are good sons. But she wants big. She wants bigger than yours."

"I can't afford that," said Nell.

Lillie shrugged. "I told her. But she doesn't believe."

After that it was Nell who went looking, with Lillie, in Lillie's white car. Lillie drove crouched forward, as if skiing. In a couple of the narrower driveways they had trouble; Lillie ran over a hosta. Nell wondered about her eyesight. Nevertheless, they found something that fit the criteria, more or less: a two-storey semi-detached with a tiny back garden and a deck, and a glassed-in breakfast nook, and three small rooms upstairs.

The sellers, two youngish men, sat on the sofa and watched the potential buyers trampling up their stairs. They'd arranged some potted plants in front of the main window – a geranium, a couple of ailing begonias – but that was the only concession they'd made. They hadn't even vacuumed. In such a market, why bother?

"Feh," said Lillie in the cellar. "This junk will go. At least it's dry. If a person was tall it would be a problem, but who's tall? For doing the laundry, it's not so bad. Upstairs, she can knock out a wall, put in a skylight, for one person it's spacious, it could be charming, you know what I mean?"

Nell and Lillie rushed into the real-estate office and put in the offer just in time. Half a day longer and it would have gone, said Lillie. Oona would pay rent: that was the arrangement she wanted, said the boys. She didn't want Nell supporting her. The rent wouldn't be enough to cover everything, but Oona didn't know that.

Nell and Oona were no longer on speaking terms; they hadn't been for some time. The boys had been the go-betweens.

It had been hard on the boys, Nell knew that. She felt sorry for them. She even felt sorry for Oona, though it took some effort. She decided she herself was not a generous person at heart. Some of her flakier friends – those into crystals and so forth – would have told her that Oona was payback for a bad thing she'd done in a previous life. They'd have said being nice to Oona was a task she'd been given. That was one way of looking at it, thought Nell. The other way was that she was a doormat.

Nell closed the deal without telling Tig. When she did tell him, he said two things: *You're crazy. Thank you.*

"You are a good person," said Lillie. She sent two bowls of hard cookies, and two notes on her flowered notepaper: one to Nell and one to Oona.

. . .

For a short while all was tranquility. Nell felt virtuous, Oona felt safer and stopped complaining about the awfulness of Nell and Tig, Tig felt less worried, the boys felt free. Nell told her friends she'd made the right decision. She enjoyed their incredulity: after all the things Oona had said about Nell – that the friends knew Nell knew she'd said, because they themselves had been the messengers – Nell buys Oona a house? What kind of a saint did she think she was?

Things needed to be fixed: with a house there's always fixing, as Lillie pointed out. There was the front porch, there was the air conditioning, there was the painting – the boys helped with that. There was the roof; you didn't get a roof done for nothing. But Oona had excellent taste, she'd always had it, and this was one of her powers that hadn't deserted her. Once she'd got her furniture arranged, you wouldn't have known the place. "She's made it like new," Lillie reported to Nell; for, like everyone else, Oona had taken a shine to Lillie, and had had her over to tea.

But the state of equilibrium did not last. Oona's health had improved at first, but now it was on the downturn. Her legs were shaky; she had trouble going up and down the stairs; she no longer felt she could walk to the corner store. The big containers for plants she'd put out on the deck were too much to water. She heard sounds at night – most likely just raccoons, though, as Lillie said, with sounds you never knew – and they frightened her. The boys put in an alarm system, but it went off once by mistake and that frightened Oona even more, so they took it out.

Maybe all this fear was her medications, said the boys. She was on a new pill, or two, or three. She didn't want to take these pills, she thought they were making her worse. In addition to that, she was convinced that she'd end up as a derelict on the street — that she'd use up her savings, that she'd run out of money, and that Nell — who was in effect her landlady — would kick her out.

"I would never do that," said Nell. But Oona thought she would.

Underneath Oona's expressions of fear was a wish that Nell would reduce or cancel the rent she was paying. One of the boys hinted at this. But Nell was running as fast as she could, financially speaking. In addition to that, she felt pushed too far. I've bent enough, she thought. One more bend and I'll snap.

The boys wanted Oona to move into an apartment — an affordable one, with an elevator. Oona couldn't decide; she couldn't climb stairs, but on the other hand elevators were constricting, like tunnels. She was working herself into a state, said the boys. She complained of insomnia. But after using up several real-estate agents and pursuing many possibilities that didn't work out, they finally found something suitable. It was a one-bedroom, small but manageable; it would be safer; it would not be too much for Oona to handle. Oona reluctantly agreed. She didn't want to move, but she didn't want to stay where she was either.

Nell called Lillie in to sell the house.

"With furniture, it's always better," said Lillie. "A person can see possibilities. And this furniture is charming." She wanted to hold an Open House, and Oona at last agreed to that. One of the boys would be there to help; the other would take her out for the day so she wouldn't have to deal with the crowds of prospective buyers. Lillie would deal with them.

As for Nell and Tig, they went to Europe — to Venice. They'd never been, they'd always wanted to go. With the money about to be freed up by the sale of the house – Oona's house, everyone now called it – they could afford the trip.

It was time for such a trip, Nell thought. The two of them needed to extract themselves from the slow grey whirlpool that swirled around Oona.

Lillie manoeuvred her white car into the driveway, parked, levered herself out. She went up the front steps, one at a time: her feet were hurting more and more. She rang the doorbell. Oona was supposed to be there to let her in so she could check everything out, get ready for the Open House, but nobody answered.

As Lillie stood on the front porch wondering what to do, the sons drove up. They too rang the bell. Then one of them – the elder – scaled the fence and climbed down via the plant containers, and looked in through the floor-to-ceiling windows of the glassed-in breakfast nook. Oona was lying on the floor.

The son kicked in the glass, cutting a vein in his leg. Oona was dead. The doctor later said she'd been dead for several hours. She'd had a stroke. A cup of tea was still on the kitchen table. The son, holding his leg and trailing blood, hobbled to the front door and let in the others. An ambulance was called; the elder son lay on the floor with his leg in the air and the younger one tried to staunch the blood with tea towels. Lillie sat on the sofa in the living room, white as a sheet and trembling. "I have never seen such a terrible thing," she said, over and over.

Which, to Nell, when all of this was reported to her later, was the first sign that something was seriously wrong with Lillie, because this was not the most terrible thing that Lillie had ever seen. Not by a long shot.

The Open House was cancelled, of course. You couldn't sell a house with so much blood on the floor. But later — weeks later, once the furniture had been cleared out — Lillie tried again. Her heart wasn't in it, though, Nell realized. She lacked her old enthusiasm, her conviction that better could come out of worse. Not only that, she was afraid of the house itself.

"The house is dark," she told Nell. "Nobody wants to live in such dark." She suggested that the bushes could be pruned.

Nell and Tig went over to the house. It wasn't dark. If anything, it was a bit too bright: bright could mean hot, in summer. Nevertheless they lopped off some branches.

"The cellar — it's full of water," said Lillie on the phone. She was upset. Tig drove over immediately. "The cellar's dry as a bone," he told Nell.

Nell had Lillie over to tea. The daffodils were in bloom; Lillie gazed out the window at them. "What do you call those?" she said.

"Lillie," said Nell, "you don't have to sell the house. Someone else can do it."

"I want to do it, for you," said Lillie. "You've had troubles."

"You think the house is dark," said Nell.

"I have never seen such a terrible thing," said Lillie. "Terrible. There was such blood."

"It wasn't Oona's blood," said Nell.

"It was blood," said Lillie.

"You think Oona's still in there," said Nell.

"You understand everything," said Lillie.

"I can take care of it," said Nell. "I know people who do these things."

"You are a good person," said Lillie, and Nell realized that Lillie was giving up, she was handing over. She was refusing to be the one who would understand, the one who would take care of everything. Nell would have to do that now, for Lillie.

Nell called her feng shui friend, who found her an expert in crystals and purification. There was a fee: cash would be preferable, said the friend. "Fine," said Nell. "Don't tell her anything about Oona or dying. I want this to be a clean read." Was Oona still in the house? Was she hindering the sale out of vengeance? Nell didn't think so. She couldn't imagine Oona doing anything so banal. But then, both of them had been guilty of equivalent banalities. The first wife, the second wife – they could have been typecast.

Tig drove Nell over to the house, but stayed outside in the car. He wasn't going to have anything to do with this. Nell let herself in with her key, and then she let in the crystal person, whose name was Susan. Susan was not a wispy sort of woman; instead she was athletic-looking, businesslike, matter-of-fact. She took the envelope with her cash payment and tucked it into her purse. "We'll start with the top floor," she said.

Susan went over the house – into every room, down into the cellar, out onto the deck. In each area she stood still, with her head tilted to one side. Finally, she went into the kitchen.

"There's nobody in the house now," she said, "but right here there's a channel where the entities come and go." She pointed to the breakfast nook.

"A channel?" said Nell.

"Sort of like a tunnel. A link," said Susan patiently. "They come into our world and then they go out of it, right here."

"This is the place where somebody died," said Nell.

"In that case, they came here on purpose because they wanted to make a quick transition," said Susan.

Nell thought about that. "Are the entities good or bad?" she said.

"They could be either," said Susan. "There are all kinds."

"If you had bad ones in the house, what would you do?"

"Put light around them," said Susan.

Nell didn't ask how a person might go about that. "Do you think the entities would mind if we closed up the channel or moved it somewhere else?" she said. This was a lot like a children's game featuring an imaginary friend. Whatever works, she told herself.

"I'll ask them," said Susan. She stood silently, listening. "They say it's all right, but they want the channel moved out into the yard. They don't want it moved too far away. They like the neighbourhood."

"It's a deal," said Nell. Even the entities had real-estate preferences, it seemed. "What do we do next?"

What they did next was a kind of circular dance, complete with some bell jingling; Susan had the bells in her purse. "There," she said. "The channel's closed. But just to make sure . . ." She took out some bundles of sage and laid them in the kitchen drawers. "That should hold them at bay for a while," she said.

"Thank you," said Nell.

It's all right now," Nell told Lillie.

"You are so kind," said Lillie.

But it wasn't all right. Lillie was still afraid of the house. There was something in it that wasn't Oona. There was something older, something darker, something more terrible. There was something that had been stirred up; it had awakened, it had come to the surface. There was blood.

Later, Nell would tell people that this must have been the first stages of Alzheimer's, or whatever it was that shortly took Lillie away from them, out of this world as she had known it. She went to a better place, however; a place devoid of the past, or of some parts of the past. In this place, several of the people she'd known long ago were still alive. Her husband was still alive. He was waiting for her to get home, she said. He didn't like her to be out by herself, he liked her to be there in the living room, with the familiar china ornaments, especially after dark.

Lillie's grown-up children made arrangements. They got a caregiver so Lillie could stay in her own house. That would be more comforting to her, they thought. She took up painting with watercolours, a thing she had never done before. The pictures she painted were bright and cheerful, filled with sunlight; they were mostly pictures of flowers. When Nell went to see her, she would smile happily. "I made some cookies, special for you," she'd say. But she hadn't made any.

Oona's house has been bought by two gay men — two artistic gay men, friends of Nell's and, as it turned out, former clients of Lillie's — who love the light that comes in on the second floor at the back. They've made a studio there. They've pulled out some walls, and added on, and put in a skylight, and redecorated. They have an unusual arrangement for their cat — a cat box that slides in and out of the wall when the cat activates it with a sensor. The cat behaves strangely in the glassed-in breakfast nook, they tell Nell: it sits and stares out the window as if it's watching something.

"It's watching the entities," says Nell, who is over having tea and admiring the renovations. "We moved them out into the yard. That's where they wanted their channel."

"What?" say the gay men. "The aunties? Don't tell me we're overrun by aunties!" They laugh.

"No, the entities," says Nell.

Then Nell tells them the story of Oona, and Tig, and herself, and Susan the crystal lady – they love the part about Nell dancing in a circle with the jingle bells – and also the story of Lillie. She changes the story a bit, of course. She makes it funnier than it seemed at the time. Also, everyone in it is nicer than they really were. Except Lillie; there's no need to improve Lillie.

The gay men like the story: it's bizarre, and they like bizarre. Also it's a story about them, since it's a story about their house. It adds character to a dwelling, to have a story attached. "We've got entities!" they say. "Who knew? If we ever sell the house we'll put it in the ad. Charming studio. Built-in cat box. Entities."

But what else could I do with all that? thinks Nell, wending her way back to her own house. All that anxiety and anger, those dubious good intentions, those tangled lives, that blood. I can tell about it or I can bury it. In the end, we'll all become stories. Or else we'll become entities. Maybe it's the same.

The Labrador Fiasco

t's October; but which October? One of those Octobers, with their quick intensities of light, their diminuendos, their red and orange leaves. My father is sitting in his armchair by the fire. He has on his black-and-white checked dressing gown, over his other clothes, and his old leather slippers, with his feet propped up on a hassock. Therefore it must be evening.

My mother is reading to him. She fiddles with her glasses, and hunches over the page; or it looks like hunching. In reality that is just the shape she is now.

My father is grinning, so this must be a part he enjoys. His grin is higher on the left side than on the right: six years ago he had a stroke, which we all pretend he's recovered from; and he has, mostly.

"What's happening now?" I say, taking off my coat. I already know the story, having heard it before.

"They've just set out," says my mother.

My father says, "They took the wrong supplies." This pleases him: he himself would not have taken the wrong supplies. In fact he would never have gone on this ill-advised journey in the first place, or – although he was once more reckless, more impetuous, more sure of his ability to confront fate and transcend danger – this is his opinion now. "Darn fools," he says, grinning away.

But what supplies could they have taken, other than the wrong ones? White sugar, white flour, rice; that was what you took then. Peameal, sulphured apples, hardtack, bacon, lard. Heavy things. There was no freeze-drying then, no handy packaged soups; there were no nylon vests, no pocket-sized sleeping bags, no lightweight tarpaulins. Their tent was made of balloon silk, oiled to waterproof it. Their blankets were of wool. The packsacks were canvas, with leather straps and tumplines that went across the forehead to cut the strain on the back. These would have smelled of tar. In addition there were two rifles, two pistols, twelve hundred rounds of ammunition, a camera, and a sextant; and then the cooking utensils and the clothing. Every pound of it had to be carried over each and every portage, or hauled upriver in the canoe, which was eighteen feet long, wood-framed, and canvas-covered.

None of this would have daunted the adventurers, however, or not at first. There were two of them, two young Americans; they'd been on camping expeditions before, although at warmer latitudes, with fragrant evening pipes smoked before cheerful blazes and a fresh-caught trout sizzling in the pan while the sunsets paled in the west. Each would have been able to turn a neat, Kiplingesque paragraph or two on the lure of wild places, the challenge of the unknown. This was in 1903, when exploration was still in vogue as a test of manliness, and when manliness itself was still in vogue, and was thought to couple naturally with the word *clean*. Manliness, cleanliness, the wilderness, where you could feel free. With gun and fishing rod, of course. You could live off the land.

The leader of the expedition, whose name was Hubbard, worked for a magazine dedicated to the outdoors. His idea was that he and his chum and cousin — whose name was Wallace — would penetrate the last unmapped Labrador wilds, and he would write a series of articles about their adventures, and thus make his name. (These were his very words: "I will make my name.") Specifically, they would ascend the Nascaupee River, said to flow out of Lake Michikamau, a fabled inland lake teeming with fish; from there they could make it to the George River, where the Indians congregated every summer for the caribou hunt, and from there to a Hudson's Bay post, and out to the coast again. While among the Indians, Hubbard planned to do a little amateur anthropology, which he would also write up, with photographs — a shaggy-haired hunter with an old-fashioned rifle, his foot on a carcass; a cut-off head, with spreading antlers. Women with bead necklaces and gleaming eyes chewing the hide, or sewing it, or whatever they did. *The Last Wild People*. Something like that. There was a great interest in such subjects. He would describe the menus too.

(But those Indians came from the north. No one ever took the river route from the west and south.)

In stories like this, there is always — there is supposed to be — an old Indian who appears to the white men as they are planning to set out. He comes to warn them, because he is kind at heart and they are ignorant. "Do not go there," he says. "That is a place we never go." Indians in these tales have a formal manner of speaking.

"Why not?" the white men say.

"Bad spirits live there," says the old Indian. The white men smile and thank him, and disregard his advice. Native superstition, they think. So they go where they've been warned not to, and then, after many hardships, they die. The old Indian shakes his head when he hears of it. Foolish white men, but what can you tell them? They have no respect.

There's no old Indian in this book – he somehow got left out – so my father takes the part upon himself. "They shouldn't have gone there," he says. "The Indians never went that way." He doesn't say *bad spirits*, however. He says, "Nothing to eat." For the Indians it would have been the same thing, because where does food come from if not from the spirits? It isn't just there, it is given; or else withheld.

Hubbard and Wallace tried to hire several Indians, to come with them, at least on the first stages of the journey, and to help with the packs. None would go; they said they were "too busy." Really they knew too much. What they knew was that you couldn't possibly carry with you, in there, everything you would need to eat. And if you couldn't carry it, you would have to kill it. But most of the time there was nothing to kill. "Too busy" meant too busy to die. It also meant too polite to point out the obvious.

The two explorers did do one thing right. They hired a guide. His name was George, and he was a Cree Indian, or partly; what they called then a "breed." He was from James Bay, too far away from the Labrador to know the full and evil truth about it. George travelled south to meet his employers, all the way to New York City, where he had never been before. He had never been to the United States before, or even to a city. He kept calm, he looked about him; he demonstrated his resourcefulness by figuring out what a taxicab was, and how to hire one. His ability to reason things through was to come in very handy later on.

"That George was quite a boy," says my father. George is his favourite person in the whole story.

Somewhere around the house there's a picture of my father himself – at the back of a photo album, perhaps, with the snapshots that haven't yet been stuck in. It shows him thirty years younger, on some canoe trip or another – if you don't write these things down on the backs of the pictures, they get forgotten. He's evidently crossing a portage. He hasn't shaved, he's got a bandana tied around his head because of the blackflies and mosquitoes, and he's carrying a heavy pack, with the broad tumpline across his forehead. His hair is dark, his glistening face is deeply tanned and not what you'd call clean. He looks slightly villainous; like a pirate, or indeed like a northwoods guide, the kind that might suddenly vanish in the middle of the night, along with your best rifle, just before the wolves arrive on the scene. But like someone who knows what he's doing.

"That George knew what he was doing," says my father now.

Once he got out of New York, that is; while there, George wasn't much help, because he didn't know where to shop. It was in New York that the two men bought all the necessary supplies, except a gill net, which they thought they could find up north. They also failed to purchase extra moccasins. This may have been their worst mistake.

Then they set out, by train and then by boat and then by smaller boat. The details are tedious. The weather was bad, the meals were foul, none of the transportation was ever on time. They spent a lot of hours and even days waiting around on docks and wondering when their luggage would turn up.

"That's enough for tonight," says my mother.

"I think he's asleep," I say.

"He never used to go to sleep," says my mother. "Not with this story. Usually he's busy making up his list."

"His list?"

"His list of what he would take."

While my father sleeps, I skip ahead in the story. The three men have finally made it inland from the bleak northeastern shore of Labrador, and have left their last jumping-off place, and are voyaging in earnest. It's the middle of July, but the short summer will soon be over, and they have five hundred miles to go.

Their task is to navigate Grand Lake, which is long and thin; at its extreme end, or so they've been told, the Nascaupee flows into it. The only map they've seen, crudely drawn by an earlier white traveller some fifty years before, shows Grand Lake with only one river emptying into it. One is all the Indians have ever mentioned: the one that goes somewhere. Why talk about the others, because why would anyone want to know about them? There are many plants that have no names because they cannot be eaten or used.

But in fact there are four other rivers.

During this first morning they are exhilarated, or so Wallace records. Their hopes are high, adventure calls. The sky is deep blue, the air is crisp, the sun is bright, the treetops seem to beckon them on. They do not know enough to beware of beckoning treetops. For lunch they have flapjacks and syrup, and are filled with a sense of well-being. They know they're going into danger, but they also know they are immortal. Such moods do occur, in the north. They take pictures with their camera: of their canoe, of their packsacks, of one another: moustached, be-sweatered, with puttee-shaped wrappings on their legs and things on their heads that look like bowler hats, leaning blithely on their paddles. Heartbreaking, but only when you know the end. As it is they're having the time of their lives.

There's another photo of my father, perhaps from the same trip as the one with the portage; or he's wearing the same bandana. This time he's grinning into the camera lens, pretending to shave himself with his axe. Two tall-tale points are being made: that his axe is as sharp as a razor, and that his bristles are so tough that only an axe could cut them. It's highjinks, a canoe-trip joke. Although secretly of course he once believed both of these things.

On the second day the three men pass the mouth of the Nascaupee, which is hidden behind an island and looks like shoreline. They don't even suspect it is there. They continue on to the end of the lake, and enter the river they find there. They've taken the wrong turn.

I don't get back to Labrador for more than a week. When I return, it's a Sunday night. The fire is blazing away and my father is sitting in front of it, waiting to see what will happen next. My mother is rustling up the baking-powder biscuits and the decaffeinated tea. I forage for cookies.

"How is everything?" I say.

"Fine," she says. "But he doesn't get enough exercise." *Everything* means my father, as far as she is concerned.

"You should make him go for a walk," I say.

"*Make* him," she says.

"Well, suggest."

"He doesn't see the point of walking just to walk," she says. "If you're not going anywhere."

"You could send him on errands," I say. To this she does not bother even to reply.

"He says his feet hurt," she says. I think of the array of almost-new boots and shoes in the closet; boots and shoes that have proliferated lately. He keeps buying other ones. If only he can find the right pair, he must think, whatever it is that's causing his feet to hurt will go away.

I carry in the teacups, dole out the plates. "So, how are Hubbard and Wallace coming along?" I say. "Have you got to the place where they eat the owl?"

"Slim pickings," he says. "They took the wrong river. Even if they'd found the right one, it was too late to start."

Hubbard and Wallace and George toil upstream. The heat at midday is oppressive. Flies torment them, little flies like pinpricks, giant ones as big as your thumb. The river is barely navigable: they have to haul their laden canoe over gravel shallows, or portage around rapids, through forest that is harsh and unmarked and jumbled. In front of them the river unrolls; behind them it closes up like a maze. The banks of the river grow steeper; hill after hill, gentle in outline, hard at the core. It's a sparse landscape: ragged spruce, birch, aspen, all spindly, in some places burned over, the way forward blocked by charred and fallen tree trunks.

How long is it before they realize they've gone up the wrong river? Far too long. They cache some of their food so they won't have to carry it; they throw some of it away. They manage to shoot a caribou, which they eat, leaving the hooves and head behind. Their feet hurt; their moccasins are wearing out.

At last Hubbard climbs a high hill, and from its top he sees Lake Michikamau; but the river they have been following does not go there. The lake is too far away: they can't possibly haul their canoe that far through the forest. They will have to turn back.

In the evenings their talk is no longer of discovery and exploration. Instead they discuss what they will eat. What they'll eat tomorrow, and what they'll eat when they get back. They compose bills of fare, feasts, grand blowouts. George is able to shoot or catch this and that. A duck here, a grouse there. A whiskeyjack. They catch sixty trout, painstakingly one by one, using a hook and line because they have no gill net. The trout are clear and fresh as icewater, but only six inches long. Nothing is nearly enough. The work of travelling uses up more energy than they can take in; they are slowly dissolving, wasting away.

Meanwhile the nights become longer and longer and darker and darker. Ice forms at the edges of the river. Hauling the canoe over the shallows, through the rushing stone-cold water, leaves them shivering and gasping. The first snowflurries fall.

"It's rough country," says my father. "No moose. Not even bears. That's always a bad sign, no bears." He's been there, or near it; same sort of terrain. He speaks of it with admiration and nostalgia, and a kind of ruefulness. "Now of course you can fly in. You can cover their whole route in a couple of hours." He waves his fingers dismissively: so much for planes.

"What about the owl?" I say.

"What owl?" says my father.

"The one they ate," I say. "I think it's where the canoe dumps, and they save their matches by sticking them in their ears."

"I think that was the others," says my father. "The ones who tried the same thing later. I don't think this bunch ate an owl."

"If they had eaten one, what sort of owl would it have been?" I say.

"Great horned or boreal," he says, "if they were lucky. More meat on those. But it may have been something smaller." He gives a series of thin, eerie barks, like a dog at a distance, and then he grins. He knows every bird up there by its call; he still does.

He's sleeping too much in the afternoons," says my mother.

"Maybe he's tired," I say.

"He shouldn't be that tired," she says. "Tired, and restless as well. He's losing his appetite."

"Maybe he needs a hobby," I say. "Something to occupy his mind."

"He used to have a lot of them," my mother says.

I wonder where they've all gone, those hobbies. Their tools and materials are still around: the plane and the spirit level, the feathers for tying dry flies, the machine for enlarging prints, the points for making arrows. These bits and pieces seem to me like artifacts, the kind that are dug up at archaeological sites, and then pondered over and classified, and used for deducing the kind of life once lived.

"He used to say he wanted to write his memoirs," says my mother. "A sort of account. All the places he's been. He did begin it several times, but now he's lost interest. He can't see too well."

"He could use a tape recorder," I say.

"Oh help," says my mother. "More gadgets!"

The winds howl and cease, the snow falls and stops falling. The three men have traversed across to a different river, hoping it will be better, but it isn't. One night George has a dream: God appears to him, shining and bright and affable, and speaks in a manner that is friendly but firm. "I can't spare any more of these trout," he says, "but if you stick to this river you'll get down to Grand Lake all right. Just you don't leave the river, and I'll get you out safe."

George tells the others of his dream. It is discounted. The men abandon their canoe and strike out overland, hoping to reach their old trail. After far too long they do reach it, and stumble along it down the valley of the river they first ascended, rummaging through their former campsites for any food they might have thrown away. They aren't counting in miles, but in days; how many days they have left, and how many it will take. But that will depend on the weather, and on their own strength: how fast they can go. They find a lump of mouldering flour, a bit of lard, a few bones, some caribou hooves, which they boil. A little tin of dry mustard; they mix it into the soup, and find it encouraging.

In the third week of October, this is how things stand:

Hubbard has become too weak to go any farther. He's been left behind, wrapped in his blankets, in the tent, with a fire going. The other two have gone on; they hope to walk out, then send help back for him. He's given them the last of the peameal.

The snow is falling. For dinner he has some strong tea and bone broth, and some boiled rawhide, made from the last of his moccasins; he writes in his journal that it is truly delicious. Now he is without footgear. He has every hope that the others will succeed, and will return and save him, or so he records. Nevertheless he begins a farewell message for his wife. He writes that he has a pair of cowhide mittens he's looking forward to cooking and eating the next day.

After that he goes to sleep, and after that he dies.

Some days farther down the trail, Wallace too has to give up. He and George part company: Wallace intends to go back with the latest leavings they've managed to locate — a few handfuls of mouldy flour. He will find Hubbard, and together they will await rescue. But he's been caught in a blizzard and has lost his bearings; at the moment he's in a shelter made of branches, waiting for the snow to let up. He is amazingly weak, and no longer hungry, which he knows is a bad sign. Every movement he makes is slow and deliberate, and at the same time unreal, as if his body is apart from him and he is only watching it. In the white light of day or the red flicker of the fire — for he still has fire — the whorls on the ends of his own fingers appear miraculous to him. Such clarity and detail; he follows the pattern of the woven blanket as if tracing a map.

His dead wife has appeared to him, and has given him several pieces of practical advice concerning his sleeping arrangements: a thicker layer of spruce boughs underneath, she's said, would be more comfortable. Sometimes he only hears her, sometimes he sees her as well; she's wearing a blue summer dress, her long hair pinned up in a shining coil. She appears perfectly at home; the poles of the shelter are visible through her back. Wallace has ceased to be surprised by this.

Even farther along, George continues to walk; to walk out. He knows more or less where he's going; he will find help and return with it. But he isn't out yet, he's still in. Snow surrounds him, the blank grey sky enfolds him; at one point he comes across his own tracks and realizes he's been walking in a circle. He too is thin and weak, but he's managed to shoot a porcupine. He pauses to think it through: he could turn around, retrace his steps, take the porcu-pine back to share with the others; or he could eat all of it himself, and go forward. He knows that if he goes back it's likely that none of them will get out alive; but if he goes on, there's at least a possibility, at least for him. He goes on, hoarding the bones.

"That George did the right thing," says my father.

A week later, while sitting at the dinner table, my father has another stroke. This time it knocks out half the vision in each eye, and his short-term memory, and his sense of where he is. From one minute to the next he has become lost; he gropes through the living room as if he's never been in such a place before. The doctors say this time it's unlikely he'll recover.

Time passes. Now the lilacs are in bloom outside the window, and he can see them, or parts of them. Despite this, he thinks it's October. Yet the core of him is still there. He sits in his armchair, trying to figure things out. One sofa cushion looks much like another unless you have something to go by. He watches the sunlight gleaming on the hardwood floor; his best guess is it's a river. In extreme situations you have to use your wits.

"I'm here," I say, kissing his dry cheek. He hasn't gone bald, not in the least. He has silvery-white hair, like an egret frozen.

He peers at me, out of the left sides of his eyes, which are the ones that work.

"You seem to have become very old all of a sudden," he says.

As far as we can tell he's missing the last four or five years, and several blocks of time before that as well. He's disappointed in me: not because of anything I've done, but because of what I've failed to do. I've failed to remain young. If I could have managed that I could have saved him; then he too could have remained as he was.

I wish I could think of something to amuse him. I've tried recordings of bird songs, but he doesn't like them: they remind him that there's something he once knew, but can't remember. Stories are no good, not even short ones, because by the time you get to the second page he's forgotten the beginning. Where are we without our plots?

Music is better; it takes place drop by drop.

My mother doesn't know what to do, and so she rearranges: cups and plates, documents, bureau drawers. Right now she's outside, yanking weeds out of the garden in a bewildered frenzy. Dirt and couch grass fly through the air: that at least will get done! There's a wind; her hair is wild, blown up around her head like feathers.

I've told her I can't stay long. "You can't?" she said. "But we could have tea, I could light a fire . . ."

"Not today," I said firmly.

He can see her out there, more or less, and he wants her to come back in. He doesn't like it that she's on the other side of the glass. If he lets her slip away, out of his sight, who knows where she might go? She might vanish forever.

I hold his good hand. "She'll come in soon," I say; but *soon* could be a year.

"I want to go home," he says. I know there's no point telling him that home is where he now is, because he means something else. He means the way he was before.

"Where are we now?" I say.

He gives me a crafty look: am I trying to trip him up? "In a forest," he says. "We need to get back."

"We're all right here," I say.

He considers. "Not much to eat."

"We brought the right supplies," I say.

He is reassured. "But there's not enough wood." He's anxious about this; he says it every day. His feet are cold, he says.

"We can get more wood," I say. "We can cut it."

He's not so sure. "I never thought this would happen," he says. He doesn't mean the stroke, because he doesn't know he's had one. He means getting lost.

"We know what to do," I say. "Anyway, we'll be fine."

"We'll be fine," he says, but he sounds dubious. He doesn't trust me, and he is right.

The Boys at the Lab

The boys at the Lab were not boys. They were young men, but not extremely young: a couple of them were already thinning at the temples. They must have been in their twenties. If you were speaking of one of them – one at a time – you would never have called him a boy. Yet, in a group, they were boys. They were "The Boys," with quotation marks around them, standing all together on the dock, some with their shirts off. They had tans: the sunlight was thinner then, the ozone layer was thicker, but still they had tans.

The boys had muscles, and also grins, of a sort that you don't see any more on men's faces. Faces like theirs date from the wartime; they went with pipes, and with moustaches. I think the boys had pipes – I seem to recall a pipe or two – and one of them had a moustache. You can see it in the picture of him.

I found the boys very glamorous. Or no: I was too young for glamour. I found them, instead, magical. They were a longed-for destination, the object of a quest. Going to see them was — in anticipation, at least — a radiant event.

The boys arrived at the Lab every spring, around the time the new leaves and the blackflies and mosquitoes appeared. They came from many directions; there were different ones every year; they worked with my father. I wasn't sure what this work involved, but it must have been exciting because the Lab itself was exciting. Anywhere we didn't go often was exciting.

We would get there in a heavy wooden rowboat, built in the five-house village half a mile away — our mother would row, she was quite good at it — or by following a twisty, winding footpath, over fallen trees and stumps and around boulders and across wet patches where a few slippery planks were laid across the sphagnum moss, breathing in the mildewy smell of damp wood and slowly decaying leaves. It was too far for us to walk, our legs were too short, so mostly we went in the rowboat.

The Lab was made of logs; it seemed enormous, though in the two photographs of it that survive it looks like a shack. It did however have a screened porch, with log railings. Inside it there were things we weren't allowed to touch — bottles containing a dangerous liquid in which white grubs floated, their six tiny front legs clasped together like praying fingers, and corks that smelled like poison and were poison, and trays with dried insects pinned to them with long, thin pins, each with a tiny, alluring black knob for a head. All of this was so forbidden it made us dizzy.

At the Lab we could hide in the ice house, a dim and mysterious place that was always bigger on the inside than it was on the outside, and where there was a hush, and a lot of sawdust to keep the blocks of ice cool. Sometimes there would be a tin of evaporated milk with holes punched in the top and wax paper stuck over them; sometimes there would be a carefully hoarded stub of butter or an end of bacon; sometimes there would be a fish or two, pickerel or lake trout, already filleted, laid out on a chipped enamel pie plate.

What did we do in there? There was nothing to actually do. We'd pretend we had vanished — that nobody knew where we were. This in itself was strangely energizing. Then we'd come out, away from the silence, back into the pine-needle scent and the sound of waves plocking against the shore, and our mother's voice calling us, because it was time to get back into the rowboat and row home.

The boys at the Lab had caught the ice-house fish, and would cook them for their supper. They did their own cooking — another unusual thing to know about them — because there weren't any women there to do the cooking for them. They slept in tents, big canvas tents, two or three to a tent; they had air mattresses, and heavy kapok sleeping bags. They horsed around a lot, or so I like to believe. There's a photo of them pretending to be asleep, with their bare feet sticking out the end of the tent. The names of the boys with the feet were Cam and Ray. They are the only ones with names.

Who took these photos? And why? My father? More interestingly, my mother? I expect she was laughing as she did it; I expect they were playacting, having fun. Maybe there was some harmless flirtation of the sort that used to go on more because everyone knew there would be no consequences. It was my mother who pasted the boys into her photo album, and wrote captions under them: *"The boys." "The boys at the Lab." "Cam and Ray, 'sleeping.'"*

THE BOYS AT THE LAB

. . .

My mother is lying in bed, where's she been for a year now. In some ways it's an act of will. She became progressively blinder, and then she couldn't go walking alone because she'd fall down, and she needed to have someone with her, one of her elderly friends; but even when the two of them would set out, arms linked, she'd trip and stumble and then they might both fall down. She got a black eye or two, and finally she broke a rib – she fell onto the nightstand beside her bed and must have spent many hours on the floor, painfully pulling herself up and falling down again, like a beetle inside a jar, trying to get herself back into the bed, and was discovered by the woman who'd been hired – over her protests – to come in during the days.

Then she became afraid to walk, although she never said so, and then she became angry at her own fear. Finally she became rebellious. She rebelled against all of it: the blindness, the restriction, the falling down, the injuries, the fear. She no longer wanted to have anything to do with these sources of misery, and so she retreated under the bedcovers. It was a way of changing the subject.

Nowadays she couldn't walk even if she tried to: her muscles have become too weak. But her heart has always been strong, and it keeps her going. Soon she'll be ninety-two.

I sit down on her right side, where her good ear is: she's stone deaf in the other. The hearing in this good ear and her sense of touch are her last two contacts with the outside world. For a while we believed she could still smell; we'd bring bouquets – scented flowers only, roses and freesia and phlox and sweet peas – and shove them under her nose.

"There!" we would say. "Doesn't that smell nice?"

She would say nothing. Throughout her life she lied less than most people, a great deal less: you might even say never. On occasions when a lie might have been called for, she would provide a silence. A mother of a different sort would have said, "Yes, that's just lovely, thank you so much." But she did not say that.

"You don't smell anything at all, do you?" I said at last.

"No," she said.

She's curled up on her side with her eyes closed, but she isn't asleep. The green wool blanket is pulled up to her chin. The tips of her fingers stick out: wizened fingers, almost entirely bone, closed into a little fist. Her hands have to be opened up and massaged, and that takes some doing because her fingers are clenched so tight. It's as if she's holding on to an invisible rope. It's a rope on a ship, a rope on a cliff – some rope she absolutely has to cling on to, so she won't fall overboard, so she can climb up.

She has her good ear against the pillow, shutting things out. I turn her head gently to the side so she can hear me.

"It's me," I say. Talking into her ear is like talking into the end of a long narrow tunnel that leads through darkness to a place I can't really imagine. What does she do in there all day? All day, and all night. What does she think about? Is she bored, is she sad, what's really going on? Her ear is the single link to a whole world of buried activity; it's like a mushroom, a brief pale signal thrust up from under the ground to show that a large network of interconnected threads is still alive and flourishing down there.

"Do you know who I am?" I say to the ear. It even looks like a mushroom.

"Yes," she says, and I know it's true: as I've said, she doesn't lie.

It's my function on these occasions to tell her stories. The stories she most wants to hear are about herself, herself when younger;

herself when much younger. She smiles at those; on occasion she might even join in. She's no longer voluble, she can't carry a plot, not all by herself, but she knows what's happening, or what happened once, and she can manage a sentence or two. I'm hampered in my task because I can play back to her only the stories she once told me, which are limited in number. She likes the exciting stories best, or the ones that show her in a strong light – getting her own way against the odds – or the ones with fun in them.

"Do you remember the boys at the Lab?" I say.

"Yes," she says. That means she really does remember them.

"Their names were Cam and Ray. They lived in a tent. There's a photo of them with their feet sticking out. Do you remember those ones? That summer?"

She says she does.

It's hard for me to picture what my mother was like at that time. No: it's hard to picture her face. Her face has had so many later versions of itself laid down on it, like sediments, that I can't seem to recover that other, earlier face. Even the photos of her don't correspond to anything I can recall. I remember her essence, however: her voice, what she smelled like, what it felt like to lean up against her, the reassuring clatter she would make in the kitchen, even the sound of her singing, because she did used to sing. She once sang in church choirs; she had a good voice.

I can even remember some of her songs, or parts of them:

Blow, blow, sweet and low, wind of the western sea;
Come from the something or other ta tum,
Over the something or other ta tum,

Blow him again to me,
While my little ones, while my pretty ones, sleep . . .

I used to think she was singing from happiness, but in reality she must have been singing to put us to sleep. Sometimes I wouldn't go to sleep, though I would pretend to. Then I would raise myself up stealthily on the pillow and peer through a knothole in the wall. I liked to watch my parents when they didn't know I was doing it. "I'm keeping an eye on them," my mother would say, of boiling eggs or baking biscuits, or even of us, her children. Simply being watched, then, had a protective effect, and so I kept an eye on my parents. It made them safe.

My older brother was restless; he had projects, he wanted to be up and doing, he had things to saw and hammer. He needed glasses of water, and then he'd want to know what time it was and how long it would be until morning. My mother must have sung her songs out of mild desperation, hoping to fence off a small portion of the evening for herself. If she succeeded, she would sit at the table with the kerosene lamp on, playing cribbage with my father.

On some evenings he wasn't there. He'd be working late at the Lab and would come back in the dusk, or he'd be away on collecting trips for weeks at a time. Then she'd be alone. She would spend the evenings reading, while the owls hooted outside and the loons mourned. Or she'd write letters to her distant parents and sisters, describing the weather and the events of the week, though nothing about her feelings. I know this because I myself received similar letters from her, once I'd grown up and moved away.

Or she'd write in her diary. Why did she bother with these diaries? She and her sister made a bonfire of their diaries the night before their double wedding, and it was a custom she kept up throughout her life. Why set words down, just to destroy them? Maybe she saved the diaries until Christmas so she could put the main happenings of the year into her Christmas messages. Then, on New Year's, she might have erased the old year and started again. She burned letters too.

I never asked her about her reason for doing this. She would only have said, "Less clutter," which would have been part of the truth – she liked to clear the decks, as she put it – but not all of it.

I can remember what the back of her head looked like while she was writing, silhouetted against the soft light of the lamp; her hair, the slope of her shoulders. But not her face.

Her legs, though – I have a clear image of those, in grey flannel slacks, but only at one time of day: late afternoon, with the sun low in the sky, the light coming in yellow shafts down through the trees and glinting off the water. At that hour we would walk along the hillside overlooking the lake to where there was an unusual object. It was a small cement plinth, painted red. It was only a lot-line marker, but at the time it seemed charged with non-human powers, like an altar.

This was where we would wait for our father to come back from the Lab. We would sit on the warm rock, where there was a patch of reindeer moss, brittle in dry weather, soft after rain, and listen for the sound of the motorboat – for this we would have to keep very quiet – and I would lean against my mother's grey flannel legs. Also her leather boots. Possibly I remember the intricacies of these boots – their creases, their laces – better than I remember her face because the boots did not change. At one moment they vanished – they must have been thrown out – but until that time they remained as they were.

This ritual – the walking along the hillside, the uncanny red plinth, the waiting, the leaning, the keeping very quiet – all of this was surely what caused our father to appear, silhouetted against the sun, getting bigger and bigger as the boat neared our dock.

Once in a while a couple of the boys at the Lab would come back with my father to our house and have dinner with us. Most likely the main part of the dinner would be fish. The only other choices were Spam or corned beef, or bacon, or – if we were lucky – something made with eggs and cheese. It was the War, anything in the way of meat was rationed, but fish were easily come by. My mother – when she still had hold of the plot – used to say that if they were expecting company she would just take a fishing rod down to the dock and make a cast or two. That was all it would take. She could catch enough pickerel for dinner in half an hour.

"Then I'd whack them over the heads," my mother would say to her later friends – her city friends – "and presto! Then we'd throw the innards in the lake, so the bears couldn't smell them." She'd be showing off, just a little: the friends thought she'd been crazy to go way up there into nowhere with two small kids. They didn't say *crazy*, though, they'd say *courageous*. Then she would laugh. "Oh, courageous!" she would say, implying that it hadn't taken courage because she hadn't been afraid.

Maybe Cam and Ray came to dinner, and had fish. I certainly hope so. The two of them are characters from a novel, a novel I've never read. I have no real recollection of them, but I fell in love with their pictures when I was twelve or thirteen. Cam and Ray were much better than movie stars because they were more real, or their photos were. I had no word for *sexier*, but they were that as well. They looked so full of life, so adventurous and amused, the two of them.

They're upstairs now, in my house. I took them into my care along with the rest of the photo album once my mother had gone completely blind.

All the photos are black and white, though the earlier ones have a brownish tinge; they cover the years between 1909, when my mother was born, to 1955, when she seems to have given up on the whole idea. Between those years, however, she was meticulous. Despite her letter-burning and diary-destroying, despite the way she covered her tracks, even she must have wanted a witness of sorts – a testament to her light-footed passage through her time. Or a few clues, scattered here and there along the trail for anyone who might be following, trying to find her.

Underneath each photo is my mother's careful handwriting, in black ink on the grey pages. Names, places, dates. At the front are my grandparents in their Sunday best with their first car, a Ford, standing proudly outside their white-sided Nova Scotian house. Then there are several aging great-aunts, in print dresses, the shadows cast by the sun deepening their eye sockets and frown lines and making little moustaches underneath their noses. My mother enters as a ribbon-covered baby, then changes to a little girl in a lace-collared dress and ringlets, then to a tomboy in overalls. The sisters and the brothers have appeared by then, and grow larger in their turn. My grandfather sprouts an army doctor's uniform.

"Did you have the 1919 flu?" I ask my mother's ear.

A pause. "Yes."

"Did your mother have it? Did your sisters? Did your brothers? Did your father?" It seemed they all had it.

"Who took care of you?"

Another pause. "Father did."

"He must have been pretty good at it," I say, because none of them died, not then.

An interval, while she considers. "I suppose he was."

She fought against her father, whom nevertheless she loved. He was a stubborn man, she used to say. He had a strong will. She told me once that she was too much like him.

Now my mother is a teenager, joking around in a line of girls at the beach, wearing suits with long legs and striped tops, arms around one another's shoulders. "*Sweet sixteen*," says this seaside girls' group. My mother is in the middle. The names are written underneath: *Jessie, Helene, "Me," Katie, Dorothy.* Then a similar one, winter this time, the girls in scarves and jackets, my mother in earmuffs: *Joyce, "Me," Kae, "Fighting the Storm."* In those early years of her photopasting, she always refers to herself as "Me," with quotation marks around the word, as if she's citing some written opinion to the effect that she is who she is.

Another view: this time she's nose to nose with a horse, holding the bridle. Underneath is written: *Dick and "Me."* The stories about the horses are popular with her now, I can tell them over and over. The names of the horses were Dick and Nell. Nell was easily spooked, and got the bit between her teeth, and ran away with my mother, and she slipped out of the saddle and might have been dragged to death, and then I would never have been born. But this didn't happen because she held on — like grim death, as she used to say.

"Do you remember Dick?"

"Yes."

"Do you remember Nell?"

"Nell?"

"She ran away with you. You held on like grim death, remember?"

Now she's smiling. In there — at the end of the long dark tunnel that divides her from us — she's off again on that wild gallop, over meadows, through orchards of apple trees in bloom, clinging to the reins and the pommel for dear life, her heart going a mile a minute with terrified joy. Can she smell the apple blossoms, in there where she is? Can she feel the air against her face as she rushes through it?

"Never leave the barn door open," her father told her. "If the horse bolts, it'll head home to the barn and you could get crushed against the door frame going through." And look, she paid attention, she didn't leave the door open, because Nell draws to a standstill in front of the barn, quivering and sweating and foaming at the mouth, eyes rolling. My mother unclenches herself, lets go of the reins, descends. Both of them calm down. A happy ending.

My mother loves happy endings. Earlier in her life — earlier in my life — any story that didn't have such an ending was shelved by her as quickly as possible. I try not to repeat any of the sad stories. But there are some stories with no endings, or none I've been told, and when I come across them in the invisible file of stories I haul around with me and produce during my visits, my curiosity gets the better of me and I pester her because I want to know what happened. She holds out, though. She's not telling.

People she loves — people her own age — a lot of those people have died. Most of them have died. Hardly any of them are left. She wants to know about each death as it happens, but then she won't mention those people again. She's got them safe, inside her head somewhere, in a form she prefers. She's got them back in the layer of time where they belong.

. . .

Here she is again, in winter clothing – a cloche hat, a coat with a turned-up fur collar, the flapper style: *"Me," Eating a Doughnut*. Some girlfriend must have taken that, during her college years. She earned those years, she worked for them, she saved up. The Depression was in full spate, so it couldn't have been easy. She chose a college far away from her home so she wouldn't be watched over and restricted by her father, who'd thought she was too frivolous to go to an institution of higher learning anyway. Then she was relentlessly homesick. This did not prevent her from speed skating.

There's a gap of several years, and now she's getting married. The wedding group is arranged on the front porch of the big white house, decorated with garlands made by her sister, the youngest of the three. That sister cried throughout the event. The second sister is part of the wedding, because she's getting married at the same time. My father in a short back-and-sides haircut stands with feet apart, bracing himself; he has a thoughtful appearance. Aunts and uncles and parents and brothers and sisters cluster together. They look solemn. It's 1935.

At this point in the photograph captions my mother stops being "Me" and identifies herself by her initials – her new initials. Or else she leaves her name out entirely.

Here comes her married life. Some of the key events are missing. The honeymoon was an escapade by canoe, a watercraft my mother had never dealt with before but soon mastered; there are however no pictures of it. Soon my brother materializes as a bundle, and then all three of them are in the woods. They live in a tent while my father builds them a cabin, in his off-hours, when he's not at the Lab. My mother does their cooking over a campfire and their washing in the lake, and in her spare time she practises archery — here she is doing it — or feeds grey jays from her hand, or makes a blur on the film as she splashes into the freezing cold lake.

The cabin was already built by the time I was born. It was board-and-batten and had three bedrooms, one for my mother and father, a small one for my brother and myself — we had bunk beds made from two-by-fours — and one for guests. Most of the views of it I have on file in my head are of the floor, which was where I must have spent most of my time: on it, or close to it. I have an audio file, as well: the wind in red pines, a distant motorboat approaching. Beside the front door was a piece of metal: my mother would hit it with a spike to announce that dinner was on the table. I can hear the sound of it whenever I choose.

That cabin is gone now. It was torn down; someone has built a much fancier house in its place.

Nevertheless, here is my mother, standing outside it, feeding a grey jay. She's far from the world of horses and Fords and floral-patterned aunts by now. The cabin can be reached only by a narrow-gauge railroad or the recently built one-lane gravel road, and after that by boat or trail. All around is the forest, scraggly and vast and bear-infested. Out on the lake — the cold and perilous lake — are the loons. Wolves howl sometimes, and when they do the dogs in the tiny village whine and yelp.

The Lab has been built by now too. It was built before the cabin was. First things first.

Cam and Ray must have been special, because there are a number of pictures of them. They appear on the Lab dock, and in their tent, and sitting on the steps of the log Lab building. In another picture they have bicycles. They must have brought the bicycles on the train with them, but why would they have done that? There was no place in the forest where you could go bicycling.

But perhaps they bicycled to the village along the raw new gravel road. That would have been a feat. Or perhaps they're on a collecting trip, somewhere with flat trails, because their bicycles are loaded with gear – packsacks, bundles, duffle bags, with soot-blackened billy tins hanging from the sides. They stand balancing the top-heavy bicycles, grinning their wartime grins. They have no shirts on, and their tans and muscles are on display. How healthy they seem!

"Cam died," said my mother once, when she was looking at these photos with me, back when she could still see. "He died quite young." She'd broken her rule about not telling unhappy endings, so this death must have meant a lot to her.

"What of?" I said.

"He had some condition or other." She has never been specific about illnesses: to name them is to invoke them.

"What about Ray?"

"Something happened to him," said my mother.

"Was he in the War?"

A pause. "I'm not sure,"

I couldn't resist. "Was he killed?" If he had to die too early, this seemed to me to be a suitable way. I wanted him to have been heroic.

But she clammed up. She wasn't going to say. One dead boy was enough for that day.

The last time my mother went through her photo album – the last time she could see it – was when she was eighty-nine. My father had been dead for five years. She knew she was going blind; I think she wanted to have one last look at everything – at herself, at him, at those years that must have seemed to her now so far away, so carefree, so filled with light.

She had to bend over so she was close to the page: not only was her eyesight failing, so were the photos. They were fading, bleaching out. She sped through her earliest life, smiled at herself among the girls in bathing suits, then smiled differently at her wedding picture. She lingered over the group picture of the boys at the Lab, gathered together on the dock. "There are the boys," she said. She turned the page: my father was gazing up at her, holding a stringer with a huge lake trout on it.

"I didn't mind catching them," said my mother, "but I drew the line at cleaning them. That was our arrangement: he always gutted the fish." They did have such arrangements – who did what. I'd grown up thinking of these as laws of nature. It was news to me that some of these arrangements had been set in place by her.

Then she mentioned something she'd never told me before.

"One summer," she told me, "an Indian came to the Lab."

"An Indian? You mean one of the Indians from the lake?" There were such Indians; they trapped and fished, and drifted by in canoes once in a while. People didn't have much gasoline during the War. Nowadays the Indians have motorboats.

"No," said my mother. "An Indian from India."

It would have been like my father to have taken on this incongruous assistant. He wouldn't have seen any difficulties for such an Indian, because there would have been none for him. Anyone who was serious about beetles was a friend of his. But what if the Indian was a vegetarian Hindu? What if he was a Muslim? There was always bacon, up there in the woods. If it was smoked it would keep for a long time, and was useful for frying things: eggs, if any, and Spam, and fish. Then you could rub the grease on your boots. What would a Muslim have done about the bacon?

"Was he nice?" I said. "The Indian?" There were no pictures of him, I was sure of that.

"I expect so," said my mother. "He brought his tennis whites. And a tennis racquet."

"Why would he do that?" I said.

"I don't know," said my mother.

But I knew. This young man from India must have thought he was going to the country — to what was meant by that word, once, in other places. He'd had in mind an English country house, where he could do a spot of shooting and riding and have tea on the lawn, and stroll among the herbaceous borders, and play some tennis.

He must have had an education to have qualified as one of the boys at the Lab, so he would have been from a wealthy and well-placed Indian family, with a lot of servants. The family would have thought him eccentric to have taken up the study of insects, but still, many of good family in England — such as Darwin — had done so in the past.

They had not however done so in a wilderness of this kind. How had this young Indian man wandered so far afield, across to a new continent and then right to the edge of the known world?

"What year was it?" I said. "Was it during the War? Was I born yet?" But my mother couldn't remember.

It was around this time — when she was still walking, when she'd begun to fall down — that she told me another thing she'd never told me before. She was having a recurring dream, she said; the same dream over and over. It frightened her and made her sad, although she didn't say this.

In the dream she was alone in the woods, walking by herself beside a small river. She wasn't exactly lost, but no one else was around – none of the people who ought to have been there. Not our father, not my brother, not me; none of her own brothers and sisters, or her friends or parents. She didn't know where they'd gone. Everything was very silent: no birds, no sound of water. Nothing above but the empty blue sky. She came to a high logjam across the river; it was blocking the path. She had to climb up on the slippery logs, hauling herself hand over hand, up and up and up, toward the air.

"And then what?" I said.

"That's all there is to it," she said. "It wakes me up. But then I have the same dream all over again."

One question to ask would be about the dream – why was she having it? I used to wonder that. But the other question – one I've thought of only now – would have to be: Why did she tell me about it?

Another strange thing. Tucked into an envelope with some loose photos of the lake, and the rowboat, and the Lab – those not selected for pasting – I found a few pages from one of her diaries. She had not burned each and every page, therefore; she had saved a few. She had chosen them, torn them out, preserved them from destruction. But why these? I studied them carefully, but I couldn't figure it out. No dramatic events had occurred, no responses of any note had been recorded. Was it a message, left so I could find it? Was it an oversight? Why save a page with nothing written on it but *"A perfectly beautiful day!!!"*?

. . .

Now it's four years later, and my mother is much older. "We live a long time," she said once, meaning the women in her family. Then she said, "After you're ninety, you age ten years for every year." She foresaw herself getting fainter and fainter, more and more papery, more and more whispery, and this is what has happened to her. She still smiles, though. And she can still hear, through the one good ear.

I turn her head away from the pillow so I can talk to her. "It's me," I say. She smiles. She doesn't say much any more.

"Do you remember Dick and Nell?" I begin. The two horses, usually dependable.

No response. Her smile flickers out. I'll have to pick another story. "Do you remember the Indian?" I say.

A pause. "What Indian?"

"The Indian who came to the Lab one year. When you were living up north, remember? He came from India. He had a tennis racquet. You told me about him."

"Did I?"

No hope for the Indian. He will not be resurrected, not today. I try something else. "Do you remember Cam and Ray? You've got some pictures of them, in your photo album. They had bicycles. Remember them?"

A long pause. "No," says my mother at last. She never lies.

"They slept in a tent," I say, "with their feet sticking out. You took their picture. Cam died young. He had a condition."

She turns her head on the pillow, closing off her good ear. She shuts her eyes. That is the end of the conversation. She's back inside, way back, back in the time of legend. What's she doing? Where is she? Is she galloping through the trees on horseback, is she fighting the storm? Is she herself again?

The fate of the boys is now up to me. Also that of the young man from India. I picture him getting off the little train, hauling an enormous leather valise, with his tennis racquet in its press under his arm. What would have been inside the valise? Beautiful silk shirts. Fine cashmere jackets. Casually elegant shoes.

He crunches downhill on the gravel, toward the village dock. Then he stands there. His dismay – which has been deepening with every mile he's travelled, through forests and more forests, past bogs where dead spruce stand knee-deep in water, black and naked as if burned, through gaps blasted out of the granite bedrock, past lakes as blue and blank as closed windows, then through more forests and more bogs and past more lakes – this dismay settles over him like a net. His soul feels the pull of the empty space before him: of the trees and trees and trees, of the rocks and rocks and rocks, of the bottomless water. He's in danger of evaporating.

Clouds of blackflies and mosquitoes are already attacking him. He wants to turn and run after the retreating train, calling to it to stop, to save him, to take him home, or at least to a city, but he can't do that.

From the Lab – not that he knows yet where the Lab is – a motorboat has set out. Not a launch, nothing fancy. A crude wooden boat, handmade. He's seen similar boats, but not in rich places. The boat grinds toward him over the flat water, which glares with the light from the descending sun. In the boat sits a man who is obviously a peasant: stubby in shape, wearing a battered felt hat, an old khaki jacket, and — he now sees — a peasant's wide but crafty grin. This is the servitor sent out to help him with his valise. Perhaps the country house with the lawns and tennis courts is concealed in the forest, around that hill, or the next one, the other one more or less like it.

The man in the boat is my father. He's been chopping wood, and after that — having bailed out the boat, which has a slow leak — he's had a short, sharp wrestle with the motor, which is started by pulling on a greasy piece of rope. He has a two-day beard; tree sap and oil darken his broad hands and splotch his clothing. He cuts the motor, leaps onto the dock, hitches up the boat in one motion, then strides toward the Indian, grimy hand outstretched.

The Indian man stands paralyzed: it's a crisis of manners. Surely he cannot be expected to shake the hand of this manual labourer, who is now welcoming him, and heaving his valise into the filthy boat, and manhandling his tennis racquet, and inviting him to dinner, and promising him a fish. A fish? What does he mean by a fish? Now my father is saying he's sure the boys will make him comfortable in their tent — a tent? What sort of tent? Who are these boys? What is happening?

I sometimes think about that Indian man and his northern ordeal. He must have gone back to India. Surely he would have high-tailed it for home as soon as he could get decently free. He would have had a story or two to tell, about the blackflies and the log-cabin Lab, and the two young barbarians with their bare feet sticking out of their tent.

I give the parts of the barbarians to Cam and Ray because I want them to have more of a story — more of a story than I know, and more than they probably had. I give them the task of jollying along the deracinated but educated Indian, slapping him on the back perhaps, telling him it will be okay, it will be fine. They'll take him fishing, give him some fly dope, tell him a few bear stories. Maybe they'll fix up a sleeping place for him inside the Lab itself, so he won't be so jittery: the first sound of a loon at night can be a shock. They'll show him their pipes; then they'll show him their bicycles as well, making a point of their own foolishness in having brought such next-to-useless vehicles into the forest so he himself won't feel like an idiot about the tennis racquet.

All of that will give them something to do. I want them to step forward, out of the ranks of the extras. I want them to have speaking parts. I want them to shine.

There they are now, set in motion. The two of them are bounding downhill to the dock at the Lab; they greet the Indian man, they take his hand and help him out of the boat. The sun is low, the clouds in the west are orangey pink: tomorrow will be a fine day, though possibly – says my father, heaving the leather valise out of the boat, then clambering onto the dock and squinting at the sky – there will be some wind.

Cam picks up the valise; Ray is lighting his pipe. Someone has made a joke. What about? I can't hear. Now all three of them – Cam, and Ray, and the elegant Indian – are walking along the dock. My father follows behind, carrying – for some reason – a red metal gas can. The red stands out brilliantly against the dark green of the forest.

The Indian man looks back over his shoulder: he alone can sense me watching. But he doesn't know it's me: because he's nervous, because he's in a strange place, he thinks it's the forest, or the lake itself. Then they all climb the hill, up toward the Lab, and vanish among the trees.

Acknowledgements

My thanks to all who helped with this book, including early readers of some of the stories, Jess Atwood Gibson and Graeme Gibson; to my agents, Phoebe Larmore, Vivienne Schuster, and Diana MacKay; to my editors, Nan Talese of Doubleday U.S.A., Liz Calder of Bloomsbury U.K., and Ellen Seligman of McClelland & Stewart, Canada; to Heather Sangster, tireless copy editor; to Lucia Cino and Laura Stenberg of O.W. Toad; to Penny Kavanaugh; to Sarah Cooper and Michael Bradley; to Coleen Quinn; to John Notarianni and Scott Silke; to Gene Goldberg; to Joel Rubinovich and Sheldon Shoib; to Alice Lima; and, again, to Eileen Allen and Melinda Dabaay.

I would also like to thank Ruth, Harold, and Lenore; Matthew and Graeme the Younger; Max, Bonnie, and Finn; Xandra Bingley;

and Paulette Jiles, who is a horse whisperer but is by no means a character in this book.

Some of these stories have appeared in the following magazines:

"The Bad News": *The Guardian*, 2005; *Playboy*, 2006.
"The Art of Cooking and Serving": *Toronto Life*, 2005; the *New Statesman*, 2005.
"The Entities": *Toronto Life*, 2006.
"The Labrador Fiasco" first appeared, in a slightly different form, as a Bloomsbury Quid in 1996. The true story related within this story may be found in its original version in *The Lure of the Labrador Wild* by Dillon Wallace, published in 1905 by Fleming H. Revell Company, and reprinted by Breakwater Books, Newfoundland, in 1977.
"The Boys at the Lab": *Zoetrope: All-Story*, 2006.

The title of this book, *Moral Disorder*, was the title of the novel Graeme Gibson was writing in 1996, when he decided to stop writing novels. I use it here with his kind permission.

A NOTE ABOUT THE TYPE

The text of this book is set in Perpetua, a typeface designed by Eric Gill and released by the Monotype Corporation between 1925 and 1932. This typeface has a clean look with beautiful classical capitals, making it an excellent choice for both text and display settings. Perpetua was named for the book in which it made its first appearance: *The Passion of Perpetua and Felicity*.